Seducing the Enemy's Daughter

JULES BENNETT

MILLS &
BOON

First published in Great Britain 2011
Large Print edition 2011
Harlequin Mills & Boon Limited,
Eton House, 18-24 Paradise Road,
Richmond, Surrey TW9 1SR

© Jules Bennett 2010

ISBN: 978 0 263 21621 9

Harlequin Mills & Boon policy is to use papers that
are natural, renewable and recyclable products and
made from wood grown in sustainable forests. The
logging and manufacturing process conform to the legal
environmental regulations of the country of origin.

Printed and bound in Great Britain
by CPI Antony Rowe, Chippenham, Wiltshire

JULES BENNETT

Jules's love of storytelling started when she would get in trouble as a child and tell her parents her imaginary friend "Mimi" did it. Since then her vivid imagination has taken her down a path she's only dreamed of.

When Jules isn't spending time with her wonderful, supportive husband and two daughters, you will find her reading her favourite authors, though she calls that time "research." She loves to hear from readers! Contact her at julesbennett@falcon1.net, visit her Web site at www.julesbennett.com or send her a letter at P.O. Box 396, Minford, OH 45653.

To Grace and Madelyn.
I followed my dream to lay the path
for you to follow yours.

One

"I'm sorry, sir, but the Tropical Suite isn't available until tomorrow."

"That's unfortunate, since I'm here now."

Samantha Donovan took a deep, calming breath, approached the registration desk and pasted on the umpteenth smile of the day. Running a high-class resort was certainly straining on her jaw muscles.

"Is there a problem?" she asked.

The tall, impossibly good-looking stranger turned his darkened gaze to her. "My room is unavailable."

Because she'd been in toe-pinching Jimmy Choo shoes all blasted day, Sam leaned an arm on the marble counter and directed her attention to the young employee at the computer on the other side of the registration desk. "Mikala, what is the problem with the Tropical Suite?"

The young Hawaiian girl punched in several keys; her hands shook as they hovered over the keyboard. "It seems Mr. Stone's reservation was entered into the computer for his check-in as tomorrow."

"But as you can see, I'm here today."

Sam didn't blame the man for having a bit of irritation to his voice; she was a bit irritated herself and had been since her father came up with this preposterous plan to make her gain his respect and a place in his company by getting their family's newly acquired Kauai resort up and running smoothly.

"Mr. Stone," Sam said with a soft yet professional tone. "I cannot apologize enough for this misunderstanding. We could upgrade your room and offer the Honeymoon Hideaway at no additional charge. I know that suite is available, because I just saw the couple off to the airport personally."

Another part of the job her father hadn't warned her about. Not only had the resort been operating at a loss, they'd had to lay off workers. Now, as manager, Sam found herself playing taxi driver, maid, occasionally a waitress in one of the three restaurants and yesterday she'd had to unclog a commode in the Sands Suite.

Not the luxurious position her father had made this job out to be. But she would persevere, no matter what daunting tasks she had to take on.

This once five-star resort was the newest piece of property owned by her father and brother. Details weren't given, but Samantha knew the takeover hadn't been pretty or easy, so she needed to use all her energy and then some to make sure the guests were happy, the staff was well paid and the grounds were kept immaculate.

No problem.

"Is the room clean?"

The guest's question snapped her out of her self-induced pity party. "Yes, sir. Mikala, please make the necessary changes in the computer and I'll show Mr. Stone to the suite myself."

The man had a garment bag over one broad shoulder, so Sam reached for the extended handle of the single piece of black luggage.

Now she could add bellboy—or bell girl— to the growing list, providing Sam a diverse and impressive résumé, if her father chose to boot her from the company for good.

"Ma'am." The gentleman's voice drifted over her left shoulder. "I can take my own bag."

Not slowing her pace one bit, Sam replied, "Guests don't carry their own luggage."

She hit the button for the elevator, glanced up to see what floor the car was on and tried her damnedest to ignore the sultry, woodsy scent of this handsome guest.

"What kind of gentleman would I be if I let you carry my bag?"

Glancing to the side, Sam couldn't help but notice how well his shoulders filled his navy business suit or how nice his golden, tanned skin looked against the dark material.

Why was this man alone? She couldn't believe a man who dripped with charm and sex appeal didn't have a busty, leggy blonde draped over his arm. Granted she'd been here only six short months, but she hadn't seen too many singles.

"What kind of hotel would I be running if I had guests take their own bags to their rooms?"

Just as the elevator dinged, he lifted a

dark brow. "I'm not going to win this fight, am I?"

She merely smiled over her shoulder as she stepped on to the empty elevator. Once upon a time the two lobby elevators had probably been full of laughing families and honeymooners, but not anymore. Sam wasn't sure what happened, all she knew was that her father had handed her this new resort and she was going to make it the best in Kauai, the world for that matter, or she would drop over dead in her Jimmy Choos trying.

The next time she contacted her father—he never contacted her—she'd bring up the fact, yet again, that in Kauai traditional resorts were going by the wayside and those with luxurious day spas or upscale Bed and Breakfasts were the only way to go. Of course, coming from her, she doubted he'd believe the new concept. Perhaps that's why the hotel had been in financial trouble before. Poor communication and/or lack of interest to upgrade in an attempt to compete with the other tourist hot spots.

If her father didn't listen, and soon, she feared they'd be caught in the same dilemma as the previous owners.

Since his wife's death, Stanley Donovan cared for nothing but himself. Samantha had been pushed to the back of his mind. Well, she was still his daughter whether he wanted to put forth the relationship effort or not.

Sam rested the bag's handle against her hip and hit the button for the penthouse floor. "Did you have a nice flight?"

"As a matter of fact, I did, considering I

have my own jet." A smile spread across his lips as he glanced down to his suitcase. "If you're the manager, why are you playing bellhop?"

"Mr. Stone—"

His dark gaze darted back up. "Brady."

"Brady," she said, instantly liking the strong, confident name, not to mention the way his coallike eyes raked over her. "Because I'm the manager, I have to fill in when and where someone is needed. By the time I would've found someone to take your luggage, I could've done the job myself. Besides, even though there was an error in your reservation, I want you to be confident that we will do everything to make your stay pleasant."

The elevator came to a halt, the doors slid open. She motioned for him to exit first.

"That's quite a speech," he told her as she stepped beside him. "You even have a pleasant, professional voice. It sounds as if you've used those same words once or twice before."

Sam swallowed the lump in her throat, inserting the key card into the slot of the only door on the floor. "Mr. Stone—"

His hand slid over hers, sending shivers all through her overworked, underappreciated body. "Brady, please."

Because she couldn't deny the low, seductive tone of his voice, Sam lifted her gaze only to find his eyes held more of a punch than his sultry voice and warm, strong hand.

Dark, rich brown eyes shielded by half-lowered lids roamed over her face, pausing at the lip she chewed on.

"Brady," she replied, cursing herself for allowing, even for a moment, emotions she didn't have time for to creep up. "I assure you, there are no problems with Lani Kaimana. We're happy to have you and I guarantee you'll have a pleasant and relaxing stay."

His bedroom eyes traveled back up her face, a corner of his full lips tipped into a smirk, but his hand remained enclosed around hers. "I'm sure it will be pleasant, but I don't know about relaxing. I'm here to work."

Sam forced herself to remember her task. She slid her hand from beneath his and jerked on the cool metal door handle. As much as she'd like to chat with Mr. Charming, she had a resort to save from despair.

"What exactly does Lani Kaimana translate to?" he asked.

"Royal Diamond." She swung the door in to reveal the spacious dark green and bright white suite. "I'm sure you'll be happier in this suite. Even though it's the honeymoon suite, it's the only one on this floor, so you shouldn't be disturbed. There's a king-size bed, a Jacuzzi, wet bar and Internet access."

Stepping across the threshold, Brady studied his surroundings, while Sam continued to study him. She'd seen plenty of men in business suits before, but as her eyes continued to roam over Brady's broad back, she couldn't recall seeing a single man who filled out a tailor-made jacket so well.

"This is amazing. The view through those balcony doors is absolutely breathtaking." Brady turned to face her. "I can't believe this room isn't booked year-round."

Sam took a step into the romantic suite, her eyes betraying her by drifting up to the king-size canopy draped with white sheers in the far corner perched on a stage just for the bed. An image flashed through her mind of this sexy, too-good-to-be-true handsome man stretched out beneath the crisp white sheets—wearing nothing but the sheet.

She looked back to Brady; a smile danced in his eyes as if he knew where her thoughts had wandered. "Yes, well, that's what we're working on," she said.

"How about if you discuss your plan of action with me over dinner?"

Stunned, yet flattered, Sam shook her head. "Brady, I appreciate the offer, but I cannot have dinner with you."

"Because you don't date guests?"

"No, because I'm too busy." Though now she would have to make a vow not to date guests. The topic had never come up before.

He cocked his head to the side. "Too busy to eat? How about if I come to your office?"

Obviously this man didn't take kindly to rejection. And Sam was pretty positive he hadn't heard a negative word from a woman in his lifetime.

"Thank you again, but I can't." Sam moved toward the door in an attempt to get away from his sexy scent and those piercing eyes before she gave in to temptation. She couldn't help but wonder just how many women fell into those bedroom eyes. "If you need anything, please just ask."

"Actually, there is one thing."

She peered over her shoulder. "Yes?"

"You know my name, but I don't know yours."

"Samantha Donovan, but everyone calls me Sam." She grinned. "I own the resort."

Samantha Donovan?

All this time he'd expected *Sam* to be a man. How could he not have known his worst enemy had a daughter? And a stunning one at that.

Brady slipped his smart phone from his

jacket pocket and punched in the number to his brother, Cade. Not having all the facts on a resort he intended to take over was unacceptable. How the hell had this vital piece of information not been caught before?

"Hello."

"Cade, why the hell didn't I know Sam Donovan was a woman?" Silence filled the other end. "I assume you didn't know, either?" Brady asked.

"I had no idea. Are you in Kauai?"

"Yes." Still astounded, Brady stood in the same spot he'd been in five minutes ago when *Samantha* had walked out the door after dropping the bombshell. "Not only that, but I was escorted to my suite by the Donovan heir herself. I thought old man Donovan had two sons, not a son and a daughter. I can't believe this."

"Why did she escort you to your room? Didn't they have a bellboy?"

"I thought that odd myself. I guess they are still not back up and running like Stanley thought they'd be." Knowing his worst enemy was faltering pleased Brady. "Sam came up with some excuse as to why she was pulling double-duty."

"Sam?" His brother chuckled. "You're already using a nickname? Sounds like you're better off than running into her uptight, arrogant brother, Miles."

The epiphany hit him hard. "Cade, you're a genius. I'll call you later."

Brady disconnected the call, more pleased now than he had been only moments ago. If he hadn't been blindsided, he would've come up with this plan before calling Cade.

Seducing this woman may prove to be a bit of a challenge, but challenges were something Brady lived for. He wouldn't be in the position he was today without taking on numerous risks.

Besides, he hadn't been lying when he'd told Sam he was here to work. She didn't need to know his agenda was to gain information from the resort's employees and figure a way to overtake this property from Stanley Donovan in one swift, surprising move.

Just as the old man had done.

Stanley Donovan had wanted Lani Kaimana for years, but waited until Brady's father had fallen ill with terminal lung cancer. Brady still couldn't believe his father was gone, but he had to push forward. His father wouldn't have wanted him to dwell on the loss but move on to gain back what had been taken.

Even though he'd had time to grieve, Brady still felt guilty about concentrating solely on business. The way he worked himself made him appear, to outsiders, as coldhearted. But he knew, deep in his heart, his father would've wanted him to do anything to gain back Lani Kaimana.

Brady had no intention of letting this beautiful piece of property remain in the hands of such a ruthless business tycoon for one second longer than necessary. He'd come here with the sole purpose of gaining information to use against the Donovan empire and he had no intention of leaving without it.

But now his agenda had changed, and he intended to work strictly on Samantha for the information.

This plan was getting better and better by the minute. Just the thought of entertaining such a sexy competitor had his heart accelerating.

He hadn't known what to expect once he arrived in Kauai. Actually, he'd planned on spying on Sam, assuming the Donovan son was running the place, but now that he knew Sam was actually Samantha, he'd have to pull out all the stops. Dinners, romantic strolls along the beach, some "accidental" one-on-one time. Oh, and of course, flowers. Didn't every romance begin with something as innocent as fresh-cut blossoms?

Seducing Sam would be a pleasure—his

and hers. He wasn't vain enough to deny the fact he could indeed keep Sam pleasured. Now all he had to do was find a way, a reason, to remain close to her. He had to gain information to take over this resort. Period.

Two

Brady examined his "honeymoon suite" closer now that he was alone. The bed was definitely the centerpiece of the room even though it was up on a platform in the corner. The white, sheer fabric draped over the four-poster demanded attention. He had no problem imagining Sam in that bed with him, and from the look he'd seen on her face, she'd been imagining the same thing. Yes, seducing her would be no problem and an added bonus.

Hopefully she'd be so consumed with her newly inherited duties, she wouldn't notice him prying into her personal and professional business.

Setting his seductive thoughts aside for the moment, Brady walked around the room. The open floor plan of the suite no doubt would have the intimacy level soaring. The Jacuzzi tub was in the opposite corner of the bed, just outside the bathroom. The tub, more than big enough for two, gleamed sparkling white with towels folded like swans around the edge of the porcelain.

A pale yellow sofa, mahogany desk and a small dinette table were all on the other end of the spacious room. The wall directly across from the entryway held an impressive set of French doors, which overlooked the vibrant blue ocean with white-capped waves.

Brady made his way over, shifted the filmy, white curtains aside and stepped onto a wide balcony overlooking the water. A soft, gentle breeze glided through the air, the scent of salt water wafted up from below and the crashing of the waves made him feel at home. Even though the decor had changed a bit throughout the hotel since he'd been here last, the romantic ambiance remained.

He'd grown up on a beach and had never gotten the love of the water out of his system. Adding to that, he'd always envisioned taking over this Kauai property.

The whole island had always been peaceful, a section of the world away from all the hustle of his daily life in San Francisco. He wished he could take some time to himself to enjoy the white sand, refreshing breeze and cooling water.

Perhaps one day he could talk Sam into relaxing on the beach with him. Of course, that would take a great deal of persuasion on his part, but he was a patient man. And if he could get her into a bikini, well, that would be worth the wait. Picturing her in nothing but strings and triangle-shaped material had him eager to put his game plan into motion.

Leaving the beauty of the land behind him, Brady stepped back into his room. He pulled his smart phone from his pocket and checked his e-mail. Nothing too pressing.

He punched in the number to his office,

hoping to catch his assistant before she left for the day.

"Stone and Stone."

"Abby, I was hoping to catch you."

"I was finishing up for the day and Cade just went home. What can I do for you, Brady?"

He pulled out the small desk chair and took a seat. "I just wanted to let you know I may be in Kauai a bit longer than expected. I'd like you to forward any calls I may receive regarding Stanley or Miles Donovan."

Abby paused, he assumed to jot down his request. "Is there anything else?"

"Not at the moment. If you need anything you can either call me or let Cade know," he said.

"We'll be just fine."

Brady laughed. "I doubt the two of you could go very long without me to be your go-between."

"I'll have you know we haven't had one argument since you left," she assured him.

"Just make sure you keep your claws in until I return."

Abby laughed. "Will do. Have a nice trip."

Brady disconnected the call, confident his business was in capable hands between Abby and his younger brother and business partner. Even though the two were always bickering like siblings, Abby was the best assistant they'd ever had.

Brady figured the two of them would finally call a truce and just get together, but so far, no. All the sexual tension in the office was really starting to get to him.

Before Brady had left, Cade had asked if he could come instead. But Brady was more than ready to get this vengeance started and knew Cade would be too soft or emotional when it came to the dealings of their late father.

And now that he'd seen Sam, well, he didn't want Cade anywhere near this siren.

Which reminded him, he needed to get the ball rolling with the seduction of Sam. God, he'd named the mission—Seduction of Sam. Oh, well, every war had a name. Right?

He picked up the hotel phone on the desk and dialed the concierge.

"Good afternoon, Mr. Stone. What can I do for you today?"

"I'd like to have some flowers delivered."

"Not a problem. Do you have a price range or a specific style in mind?"

Brady thought for a moment. Sam needed something to make her smile, to make her stop and think of only him. "I'd like a large arrangement of exotic flowers. The price doesn't matter. I want the most extravagant, colorful arrangement this lady has ever seen."

The young male on the other end chuckled. "Yes, sir. Do you have an address and name of the recipient?"

"I want the arrangement delivered to Samantha Donovan in her office here."

"Oh, well." The man stumbled over his words. "We'll get right on that, Mr. Stone. What would you like the card to say?"

Brady relayed the message he wanted, had the charge billed to his room and thanked the helpful employee.

Now all he had to do was wait.

In the short time he'd talked with Sam, he already knew she was too nice not to thank him personally. Hopefully she would come up to his room and do it face-to-face. That would gain him some of the alone time he needed.

With the first step of his plan already in play, Brady pulled his laptop from his suitcase and decided to get some work done.

After all, destroying every last Donovan was going to take some time. He almost hated that someone as angelic-looking as Sam had to get mixed up in this. After all, she may be a total innocent, but she was a Donovan.

And the Donovan's were responsible for the downfall of his father's empire.

Don't forget to take time for yourself.

Sam read the card once, twice. Okay, at least three times before she smiled and realized who'd sent the most obscene amount of flowers she'd ever seen.

She'd come back to her office after taking care of a minor kitchen-staff argument to check her messages. But her desk had been hidden beneath a tall crystal vase with striking flowers in various vibrant shades.

Sam hated the fact she immediately smelled each and every bud. She'd never received flowers before and this was a heck of a way to start her collection.

On a sigh, Sam knew she needed to take a moment and thank the man behind the impressive, not to mention expensive, bouquet. Could something this large and exquisite be called a bouquet?

Even though her Jimmy Choos were still biting into her little toes, she forced the pain aside and made her way to the top floor. She really didn't have the time in her hectic schedule to talk with Brady Stone, not that she minded thanking him, but she knew their next conversation wouldn't be a simple thank-you.

He'd try to get her to dinner again. And, once again, she'd turn him down. No matter how she desired to give in, she would not allow her mind to be muddled with a smooth talker. She'd learned her lesson long ago where smooth, charming men were concerned.

Once in front of the honeymoon suite, Sam smoothed a hand down her pale pink designer suit and tapped on the door. When the door swung open, Sam had to focus on breathing.

Brady had taken off his jacket, rolled up his sleeves to expose tanned, muscular forearms, unbuttoned three—she counted them—buttons of his shirt and stood holding on to the edge of the door with a wide, knowing smile on his face.

"Samantha. Please come in."

Because she knew it was rude to refuse, she stepped inside. The man had been in this overly spacious room for only a few hours and already his masculine scent enveloped her. He'd made the room his own by setting his laptop up on the desk, a pair of Italian leather shoes sat near the foot of the bed and his clothing hung in the open closet area.

Without any effort on his part, he'd already made a lasting impression. She had no doubt he left a lingering impact on all the ladies he encountered.

"I want to thank you for the flowers." Lacing her fingers together, she turned to face him as he closed the door. "I have to say I've never seen quite an arrangement."

With his hands in his pockets, he offered her a wry grin. "How did you know I sent them?"

Sam rolled her eyes. "Well, let's see. You're

the only man in the past six months to ask me out. Other than my father, my brother and the employees here, I don't even talk with men, so I did the whole process of elimination thing." Feeling a bit flirty, she added, "Plus, I'm just smart."

Brady's soft, soothing chuckle settled in the crackling air between them. "I like a woman who has brains behind all her beauty. However, I can't believe I'm the only man to ask you out in the past six months."

Oh, he was good.

"Believe it. I've been too busy working to socialize."

He took a step closer, then another. He came so close, in fact, Sam had to lift her gaze to hold his. Brady was taller than she'd first realized. At five foot six, Sam hadn't had to tip her head for too many men, especially when she wore her heels.

"All the more reason for you to have dinner with me and take an hour to yourself." He brushed a strand of hair from her shoulder. "It's the least you could do after I sent you flowers."

Sam smiled. "Are you trying to guilt me into having dinner with you?"

"Only if it's working," he said, stroking a finger down her cheek.

She eased out of his reach. "You like to touch, don't you?"

His hand lingered in the space between them. "Problem?"

"I—I'm just not used to it, that's all."

Again, Brady grinned, reaching for her face. "I bet you aren't used to stuttering around a man, either, but you're doing a nice job of it."

She swatted his hand. "I most certainly am not."

Heat rose to her cheeks. Sam knew she needed to get out of this room before she made a complete fool of herself.

"Don't get your back all up," he said, dropping his hand. "You actually gave my self-esteem a boost."

Sam laughed. "I'm sure you really needed the extra confidence."

His grin widened and she found herself mesmerized by his perfect white teeth.

"A man always needs confidence. Especially when getting turned down by a beautiful woman."

Yup, he was smooth. More than likely

he'd had his fair share of experience wooing women. And she seriously doubted he'd been turned down by too many, if any.

"I'm sure you'll find plenty of ladies at the resort or on the island to keep you occupied." She cocked her head to the side. "I thought you were here to work?"

He shrugged. "That doesn't mean I can't enjoy the company of a beautiful, sexy woman."

His compliment swept through her like a cool, gentle breeze, leaving goose bumps all over. She didn't want to be charmed by him—or anyone for that matter—but she found herself melting with each word he spoke.

What happened to not getting sucked in by smooth-talking men?

She cleared her throat. "Well, I'm sure with your confident attitude, you'll find someone to occupy your free time."

Brady threw his head back and laughed. The rich, robust sound vibrated through the air, through her, reaching each and every nerve she had, making them tingle.

"I think you just called me arrogant."

Heat rose to her cheeks once more. She'd definitely overstayed her allotted time. "I most certainly did not. Now, if you'll excuse me, I need to return to work. Thank you for the flowers."

He closed the gap between them, coming to stand inches from her. "I apologize if my words upset you." He reached up, stroked her jawline with the pad of his thumb. "I can't help but think you're too busy taking care of this resort and not yourself."

Sam stepped back, unable to think when such a potent man was touching her. She swallowed the lump in her throat. "I'm taking care of myself just fine. Thank you for your concern."

Just as she turned to go, he spoke. "If you change your mind about dinner, let me know."

Throwing a grin over her shoulder, she nodded. "Thanks again, but no. Have a nice evening, Mr. Stone."

Three

She'd purposely used the more formal name to prove to him, and to herself, she was indeed a professional. Making time for anything other than business was simply inconceivable.

As she stepped from his suite into the elevator, she knew she would have to watch herself for the duration of his stay. A man like Brady Stone could be easily led on and

Sam wasn't about to be the one to stroke his ego. Nor was she about to stroke anything else of his.

She hadn't lied when she'd said she was too busy to have dinner. Just as the elevator dinged on the bottom floor, her stomach growled, betraying her former decision. She'd grab a pack of crackers from her emergency stash in her desk drawer and get back to work. She'd already used up enough of her time chatting with Mr. Desirable Businessman.

No way would she allow this charming, ever-so-sexy man to sway her judgment toward men—correction, toward powerful, cocky men.

After years of being under her father's controlling thumb and always trying to compete with her brother, Samantha had had enough of being overpowered. She didn't want or need a man. Being alone served her purpose in life just fine. Besides, being a career businesswoman didn't leave much time for a love life. She was still young. If she chose to have a love life, she could. But right now, she didn't even have time to think about companionship, much less jump into a relationship.

So why did her face still tingle where he'd briefly touched her, caressed her? Allowing a strange man, who just happened to be passing through her resort, affect her in such a way was just absurd and something she didn't have the time for.

Yes, he was sexy. Yes, he was smooth. And, all right, yes, she was attracted. But that was it. Nothing could come between her and her goal to please her father.

Chin high, shoulders back, Sam breezed through the lobby, pleased to see people checking in at the registration desk. If her father would only let her take the reins, she had no doubt the resort would be booked year-round. Unfortunately, she was still under his thumb.

Why couldn't her father see her for the savvy woman she'd become? Sam hated the strain they'd always had on their relationship.

Each time she spoke to him, she hated the urge she had to call him sir. Nothing was casual and Sam always felt their conversations were solely about business. What few conversations they had. Every time she tried to talk to her father, he came up with some excuse as to why he didn't have time. There was always a meeting, always a client or always an employee in his office.

In short, there was always something or someone that came ahead of Sam. She should be used to it, but in fact, she wasn't. She didn't want to get used to the idea her own father put everything ahead of her.

Feeling the start of a headache, Sam made her way through the lobby, down the wide, marble-lined hallway and into her cozy office. She'd purposely chosen an office at the end of the hall so she could concentrate on work and not be disturbed unless absolutely necessary.

Though since coming here six months ago she hadn't spent too much time inside these four walls. The majority of her time had consisted of catering to guests and making sure all her employees were happy. That is, the employees they had left.

Just before her father purchased the resort, the previous owner had had so much financial trouble they'd had to lay off fifty workers. Not only did the layoff put a strain on the employees who were still here, but the ones that were let go were hardworking and desperately needed.

Sam had each of their names and contact information. And just as soon as this resort was out of the red, she intended to bring them all back...if they hadn't gone elsewhere.

Sam's eyes focused in on the vase of vibrant flowers that still adorned her desk, reminding her of the man she was trying her hardest to block out. She moved the arrangement to the small mahogany table in the corner.

Taking a seat at her desk, she opened the top drawer and pulled out a bottle of aspirin. After taking three, she slid out of her shoes and wiggled her toes until she felt each one crack. She actually thought she heard them sigh with relief.

She tugged open her bottom drawer to reveal her junk stash and grabbed a pack of peanut butter and cheese crackers. She knew she'd have orange crumbs all over her suit, but she just loved these little things.

After popping one into her mouth, she got to work checking this week's numbers and comparing them to last week. Unfortunately, the hunger headache had yet to ease up. She really shouldn't go so long without eating.

There was just so much to be done, but she had to concentrate on one task at a time or she'd become overwhelmed and never accomplish a thing.

Closing her eyes, she leaned her head back against her leather chair and polished off the rest of her snack. With her career teetering on a fine line as far as her father was concerned, she didn't have time to take breaks—regardless of hunger or headaches.

She tried to concentrate on her breathing, on the plush carpet beneath her bare feet, on the sweet fragrance wafting from the flowers. On anything other than the fact her head felt like a volcano ready to erupt.

Moments—perhaps several—passed when a knock sounded on her door. On a groan, Sam lifted her eyelids, blinking against the harsh light.

"Come in."

Her door opened, but instead of seeing a person, she saw a stainless-steel serving cart slide through the opening. Sam jerked upright in her seat.

"What's all this?" she asked as the head chef of their high-class restaurant stepped through the door behind the cart.

"Dinner." The middle-aged man smiled, lifting the silver lid to reveal one of her favorite dishes. "The special of the day, Ms. Donovan. Seared, toasted-macadamia-nut mahi with citrus aka-miso sauce."

Sam's mouth watered at the sight of the crusted filets. "But I didn't order anything."

"No, but Mr. Stone did. Should I just leave this cart here or would you rather have it over there?"

Still speechless, Sam pushed back from her desk and stood, brushing off the inevitable orange crumbs. "Thank you, Akela, I can take it."

"Enjoy your evening, Ms. Donovan." He smiled and closed the door behind him.

The strong, mouthwatering scent drew Sam to the serving cart. She pulled off another silver lid and sucked in a breath when she saw her favorite dessert, lemon cake.

Her eyes darted to the oversize arrangement in the corner, then back to the tempting dinner. She couldn't stop the smile from spreading across her lips, just as she couldn't stop herself from going back to her desk to call Brady and thank him once again for his kindness.

Just as she reached for the phone, it rang.

Thinking the caller on the other end was Brady making sure his surprise arrived, she lifted the receiver, ready to offer her gratitude for the meal, but reiterate the fact she was too busy to socialize.

"Sam Donovan," she answered, still smiling.

"Samantha."

Her father's commanding voice, calling her by her full name, wiped the smile off her face just as sure as if he'd slapped her. It sounded nothing like the smooth way Brady had said her name earlier.

Her spine stiffened, her sweaty palm gripped the phone. A business chat with her father was not what she needed right now.

Too bad her pain medication hadn't taken effect yet.

"Dad, what can I do for you?"

"I haven't heard from you in a week. What is the status of my resort?"

She hated how his voice always sounded so demanding, so cold. But even more, she hated how he referred to Lani Kaimana as "his resort." Weren't they a family? Sam knew if Miles were here in her place, their father would be a bit more considerate.

Sam walked around the edge of her desk and sank into her chair. The stiff leather groaned, mimicking her reaction to this unexpected phone call.

"I was just getting ready to cross-reference the numbers from last quarter and forward them to you. If you'll give me an hour, you'll have them."

An impatient sigh filtered through the

phone. "Samantha, the day is nearly over. I expected the report this morning."

"I've been busy today and I just now got a chance to sit in my office and pull up the spreadsheets."

Her father's sigh filtered through the phone. "I'm not interested in your excuses. Is there anything else I should be aware of?"

Her gaze focused first on the flowers, then the dinner. She refused to admit her mind and her time had been spent on a handsome businessman passing through. That would definitely not sit well with the business tycoon on the other end of the line.

"No, there is nothing else you should be informed of."

A knock on her door jarred her from her thoughts.

"I'll be waiting on that report, Samantha."

Listening to her father's edgy tone, she watched as Brady poked his head in. She motioned for him to hold on.

"I'll get it right to you," she assured her father. "If there's nothing else, I have someone in my office waiting to talk to me."

"I'll check back later in the week."

As usual, he hung up without a goodbye. Sam knew he didn't even treat his business rivals this rudely, so why did he act so cold toward his own daughter? Why did Miles deserve all the praise, all the love? And why did she always let her father's hurtful tone and words get to her?

She should be used to this. After all, she'd been treated like the black sheep for more than twenty years now.

Was it her fault her mother died? Was it her fault she looked exactly like Bev Donovan? According to her father, yes.

"Bad time?" Brady asked from the door.

Sam shook her head and smiled. "Perfect timing, actually. I was just getting ready to call you and thank you for the dinner."

He stepped into her office. "May I close the door?"

"Sure." Sam came to her feet, clasped her hands in front of her and hoped she came across as professional and that professional side hoped he wouldn't pursue a date. The woman in her hoped he did. "Looks like you're getting dinner with me after all."

"No, this is just for you." He motioned to the cart. "I do want to take you out, but I know you're busy. At least this way you may be forced to eat."

How could a woman's heart not melt at that? The man was not pushing his way to get what he wanted, he was genuinely concerned for her welfare.

Sam took in Brady's casual appearance from his khaki pants to his mint-green polo shirt. She'd thought the suit was impressive, but the way his cotton shirt stretched across his shoulders and chest made her rethink her original thoughts. What would he look like without a shirt?

"Are you okay?" he asked, bending down to look her in the eye. "You're looking a bit pale. Do you have a migraine?"

"Yes, but I'm fine."

Brady moved around the side of her desk,

studying her face. "Why don't you sit down and I'll bring the food to you?"

Before she could protest, his firm hands settled on her shoulders, easing her back into her seat.

"Brady, I appreciate everything you've done, but I have to get a report to my father and I'm sure you have better things to do."

He made his way across her office and wheeled the cart closer to her desk. "Your father won't care if you eat, and I have nowhere else I'd rather be."

Sam wiggled her mouse to wake up her computer. "I need to get this report cross-referenced and sent to him within the hour. After I'm done, then I'll eat."

Brady frowned. "Anything I can do to help?"

Sam tilted her head. "I can handle it on my own."

"Is that your polite way of asking me to leave?"

Coming to her feet, she smiled. "I don't mean to be rude, but I am rather busy."

He spread his hands wide and shrugged. "Since I arranged this nice meal, it's my duty to make sure you eat it. I'll just have a seat over here and wait for you to finish."

She didn't have time to question his actions. If he wanted to keep her company, that was fine with her, so long as he didn't interfere with her work. Besides, she kind of liked the idea of someone worrying about her. When was the last time that had happened?

Before her mother died. Before her world

changed. Before she was forced to grow up before she was ready.

Having Brady's attentiveness somehow made her spirits lift. The allure of having a perfectly handsome stranger take notice may be cliché, but it was also downright thrilling. Perhaps she should take the time to enjoy Brady while he was here if only she could add extra hours in the day.

While Sam worked, Brady sat across from her desk with his long legs extended, ankles crossed. He'd tipped his head back and laced his fingers over his flat abdomen. Even though he wasn't exactly looking at her, his presence was overpowering. His masculine scent combined with the dinner he'd ordered made her fingers fly across the keyboard. She wanted to take just ten minutes to herself and enjoy the dinner. And the man, if she so chose.

She checked and double-checked the numbers before sending them on to her father. Finally, she pushed back from her keyboard, tilting her head from side to side to work out the kinks.

"All done."

Brady's gaze came back to hers as he straightened in his seat. "Now will you eat?"

"Yes."

He quirked a dark brow. "Promise?"

Sam cleared a space on her desk, while Brady gathered dinner. He placed the main dish in the middle of her desk and grabbed the bottles of water from the cart. But instead of taking a seat, he went to the arrangement in the corner, plucked out an exotic purple flower and handed it to her.

"I would put the vase in the middle for a little romance, but I wouldn't be able to see you."

Sam took the flower he'd extended to her. "I didn't know a dinner for one could be romantic."

With his charming, killer smile, Brady took a seat across from her. "You're not alone yet. Don't ruin my romantic gesture."

His matter-of-fact tone sent shivers through her. "You're so determined to spend time with me when I've made it clear I'm too busy to socialize. Don't get me wrong, I'm flattered, but I feel like you're wasting your time. I'm not even sure I could spare two minutes."

Brady shrugged. "It's my time to waste.

But I see this as time well spent. When I see something I like, I go after it. You strike me as a woman who does the same."

She eyed him over the food. "You're right. I do."

And she wanted Lani Kaimana to be the best tourist attraction on the island of Kauai. If only she could get her father to see things her way and listen to her ideas. Or just listen to her, period.

Too bad Brady Stone had entered her life at this particular point in time. She'd love to throw caution to the wind and see where this harmless flirtation led. Perhaps, once her life settled—please, God, let that be soon—she could afford to indulge in some Brady time.

True, she never wanted a serious relationship

again, but she had a feeling Brady wasn't a long-term kind of guy. A man with so much sex appeal more than likely stuck to one-nighters.

What would it be like to be held by those strong arms? What would it be like to ignore what was right and proper? Would she be able to let her stiff, boring lifestyle go and see where her desires led?

Like everything else in her life, she could only fantasize. Until she claimed her rightful place in her father's company, she couldn't indulge in any desires. No matter how her body ached.

Four

Brady couldn't believe his luck. Well, luck only played a small part. He had to give proper credit to his charm and Sam's moment of weakness. He loved when a last-minute plan came together.

Still smiling, Brady stepped into his suite, pulled his phone from his pants pocket and dialed his brother.

Cade answered on the first ring. "Hello."

"You have no idea how close I just came to uncovering all the ammunition we need." Strutting over to the French doors, Brady took pleasure in watching the waves crash against the sand. Much like Mr. Donovan's business would come crashing to an abrupt halt in the very near future.

"What happened?" Cade asked.

"I had a very nice dinner sent to Ms. Donovan's office. When I stopped by to make sure she'd received it, she was getting ready to send the report." Brady breathed in the fresh, floral scent of the island. "I hung around by using the excuse that I wanted to make sure she ate. She never second-guessed me. I'd say I'll have that information we need within a week."

Cade let out a low whistle. "That is some

fast work, brother. And you claim I work fast with the ladies."

Brady's eyes darted to the four-poster bed in the corner; yet another image of Sam sprawled out between the silky sheets stirred his emotions. "Nothing went on between me and Sam, I just happened to be in the right place at the right time. Unfortunately, I wasn't able to get close enough without arousing suspicion."

"You've been there two days," Cade said. "I'll say you're making remarkable progress. Do you really think you can get those numbers within a week?"

Making his gaze focus back on the dark, mostly deserted beach, Brady thought of the petite blonde down in her office. He wouldn't let his hormones hinder his business dealings.

"Yes."

"Fantastic. May I ask how you were so close to the report?"

"I was in Sam's office and she had a migraine."

Brady ignored the lump in his throat as a twinge of guilt flashed through him at taking advantage of her in a moment of weakness. But then hadn't her father taken advantage of his during a moment of weakness? Turnabout was fair play…and all that.

"She needed to get her report to Stanley and I offered to help."

Cade chuckled. "Man. Too bad she didn't let you send it."

"When it comes to her business, she wants

total control." Something he had to admire. "She's a Donovan, after all. Even though I've only seen her sweet, angelic demeanor, she may very well be like her old man beneath the surface. And I'm just attracted enough not to want to see the ruthless side of her."

"I have a feeling when she finds out who you are and why you're giving her so much attention, you'll be seeing more than ruthlessness." His brother laughed. "Call me if you uncover anything else. And I don't mean Ms. Donovan herself."

Brady disconnected the call, cutting off his brother's continuous chuckle.

Brady wanted nothing more than to retrieve those numbers and get them back to Cade, but seducing Sam would take time and patience. Two things he didn't possess.

The Donovans had only been in control for six months. Six months ago when Brady's father had been battling lung cancer and struggling to keep his cooperation from going under, Stanley Donovan had swooped down like the vulture he was and took Lani Kaimana.

Stanley had always been known as a callous businessman. And from the conversation he'd overheard between Sam and her father, Brady figured Stanley had no problem being a menace to his own daughter.

Brady had seen the look of defeat when she'd hung up the phone, giving him the feeling that old man Donovan was not only a shark with competitors, but also a class A jerk with his family.

But none of those facts or images negated

that Brady and his brother had a job to do and until Lani Kaimana was back in the Stone family, Brady wouldn't back down from seducing Samantha.

Soft white sand slid between his bare toes as Brady strolled along the pristine beach between Lani Kaimana and the Pacific Ocean.

In a way, Brady couldn't fault Stanley Donovan for taking this bit of property. Who wouldn't want to own a piece of paradise and make money from it in the process? But what he did fault Stanley for was taking advantage of a sick, dying man, stealing a resort from his floundering company and aiding in the possible demise of an empire.

Hands fisted at his sides, Brady crushed the sand beneath his feet with each step.

With Brady's father gone, Stanley's reign over the Stones would end. Brady and Cade were young strong men who wouldn't be run over by a shark like Sam's father.

A gentle breeze floated along the water, sending whitecaps ruffling to the shoreline. This was the perfect weather for a romantic walk on the beach. Lately when he thought of romance, his mind immediately drifted to Sam. Of her sweet, innocent smile. Her sassy yet flirty mouth. The way her curvy, petite body looked in her clean-cut suits.

She was a woman meant for romance, for long walks along beaches just like this, for evenings spent in five-star restaurants. Not for running herself ragged to appease an ass of a father.

No romance, he told himself. The breathtaking ambiance of the evening had muddled his mind. His reason for being here was pure business. Nothing more.

Then as if his fantasy and dreams came to life, Samantha Donovan was standing just ahead of him. She still had on her perfectly pressed suit, but she held her shoes by the strap, dangling from a finger at her side.

Her long golden hair floated and danced around her shoulders as she stared out onto the horizon. As Brady approached—thanking God for this stroke of luck—he wondered what thoughts were running through her head.

Did she have worries, doubts? Was she taking a break from her hectic position?

"Beautiful, isn't it?" he asked as he came to her side. When she turned to look at him, she jerked back as if she realized he wasn't talking about the orange-and-pink sunset.

She quickly masked her surprise by turning back to the water. "I don't get out here often enough."

"You really should. The fresh scent and evening breeze will ease your mind and make you forget all your troubles."

She cast him a sideways glance. "I doubt that."

With a deep sigh, Sam turned in the opposite direction and began walking. Brady didn't wait for an invitation, he simply fell into step beside her.

When she glanced over, he smiled. "It seems a waste to walk on this beautiful beach alone, especially with a sunset as breathtaking as that one."

"Do your smooth moves normally get you the ladies?"

His grin widened at her bluntness. "Always."

The soft laughter he'd come to expect from her floated along the breeze and warmed a spot deep within. Brady didn't want to be warmed by her, he wanted information he could use to crush her family…even if that meant her. He couldn't help who got caught in the crossfire.

"So what are you doing out here?" he asked. "I didn't take you for the type to take breaks."

"I started feeling claustrophobic in my office and needed to do some thinking. I'm still working," she assured him as she tapped the side of her head. "I'm just doing it in here."

The water lapped up around their bare feet, splashing up onto her shapely calves and wetting the folded edges of his khaki pants.

To onlookers, they probably looked like a couple out for a romantic stroll. And hopefully that's how Sam would see his presence, but in reality, he was laying the groundwork for destruction.

"You know the old saying about all work and no play?" he kidded.

She stopped, turned to him. "Why do I have the feeling you get plenty of play in?"

A strand of her fair hair came around and

clung to her pink, glossy lips—her kissable lips. With the tip of his finger, he swept the hair aside.

"Maybe because I do." He watched her pale blue eyes widen with acknowledgment. "Maybe if you added a little more playtime into your life, you wouldn't be so stressed."

Her defiant chin tilted. "I happen to love what I do and if I wanted to play, I would. I can take an hour to enjoy life."

"Fine, then. When you want to forgo some work and see what else life offers, come find me." He turned, but glanced over his shoulder. "Oh, Samantha, playtime with me takes more than an hour."

He strolled off, literally into the sunset, and let her chew on that tantalizing thought.

* * *

Sam strode through the open lobby, inhaling the refreshing salt water of the early morning. If only her life were as sunny and bright as the sunshine beaming in through the doors and windows.

After a meeting with the disgruntled grounds crew, Sam had finally appeased them by explaining that a new budget was being looked over with all employees of Lani Kaimana in mind.

She did not, however, mention the fact that the new budget she was looking over wouldn't allow for too many raises until she could see how well the resort operated since switching ownership.

Unless her father listened to her, there would be no turning this resort around. He'd purchased the piece of property when it was operating at a loss, something they couldn't fix overnight.

She knew her father trusted her or she'd never be here to begin with. So why couldn't he also entertain her ideas?

Just as she turned toward her office, she saw Brady. She hadn't had much time to think of him this morning, but she'd spent plenty of time last night tossing and turning between her lonely sheets.

She took a moment to appreciate such a fine specimen of man. And, considering he wasn't looking her way, she allowed herself the satisfaction of raking her gaze over his broad, muscular body.

His crisp white polo shirt did amazing things to his golden, sun-kissed biceps.

And the way his faded denim covered his long legs as he ate up the ground made her wonder why she'd never noticed a man this way before.

Allowing her eyes to linger longer than necessary only made her heart beat faster.

Was this just a case of good old-fashioned lust? Did she just find Brady Stone appealing because he was a stranger passing through? Because he'd given her flowers, a nice meal and was there to comfort her when she'd not felt well?

Oh, and the walk on the beach. Planned or not, that had been the most romantic moment of her life. And that proved how pathetic a life she'd been living.

So, why now? Why *this* man?

Before she could answer her own questions,

Brady turned his head. His eyes locked with hers and a knowing grin spread across his face.

Damn. She'd been caught staring.

Oh, well, she couldn't undo the damage now. With her shoulders back, chin up, Sam made her way toward him.

"Good morning," she greeted with a smile.

Brady nodded, offering a warm smile of his own. "Morning."

"I forgot to thank you again for the flowers, dinner. When I ran into you last night, my mind was elsewhere." She kept her smile going, not a hardship when looking at such a magnificent man. "Are you still enjoying your stay?"

"So far."

Another happy guest. "If there's anything I can do to make your visit more pleasant, don't hesitate to ask."

His grin kicked up a notch; a naughty gleam twinkled in his chocolate eyes. "I bet I can come up with something. Is that an open-ended invitation?"

She'd walked right into that one.

The way he looked at her—as if he knew where her thoughts had traveled since meeting him—made her palms dampen. Add mind reading to his impressive personal résumé.

After their few short conversations, she should've known where his mind, and other body parts, would go with her innocent comment. He was a guy, after all.

"I do have a tight schedule," she told him,

hoping she sounded professional and not like a nervous schoolgirl. God, couldn't she make up her mind? "I'd be willing to accommodate your needs. I mean—"

He leaned into her ear. "I know what you mean, Sam." Easing back, he smiled. "When can I expect you to...accommodate me?"

Sam glanced around the nearly empty lobby. "Umm..."

Brady eased back and chuckled. "How about we start with a dinner *not* in your office?"

She so wanted to say yes. Did she dare take some time for herself? "I don't know, Brady."

"We already shared a romantic walk in the sunset," he reminded her. "Dinner isn't nearly as romantic as that."

He had her there. Besides, the man was just passing through on business. What could one meal hurt? She wasn't going to start a time-consuming relationship with him.

"Are you free tonight?"

"Absolutely. I'll take care of all the arrangements." He reached out, easing a strand of hair from her shoulders. "Meet me in my suite at six."

Before she could tell him she couldn't possibly meet him that early, he'd walked away. And Sam recalled the rule she'd recently made about dating guests. Oh, well, she'd never been a rule breaker, so doing it once wouldn't hurt.

She watched him cross through the lobby and exit into the breezy summer day. Dear

Lord, the man looked just as good going as he did coming.

Sam forced herself to concentrate on the rest of her hectic workday, but her mind betrayed her. Instead of figuring out how to bring more tourists to her father's newly acquired resort, all she could think of was how long she'd gone without sex.

And why was she even thinking about sex? It wasn't as if she were going to be intimate with Brady tonight or anything. She didn't even know him. But he was clearly interested in her and that had her thinking of the two of them tangled between sheets.

Sex. Even the word hadn't been on her mind since trying to gain her father's respect and a place in his company. She'd put all her personal desires aside in order to concentrate on her career.

Her whole life, Sam had wanted to be important to her father. Her mother had passed away years ago, leaving shattered, five-year-old Sam and eight-year-old Miles behind to be raised by a business mogul who knew nothing about raising little girls. Good news for Miles.

She'd gotten through her life just fine on her own and she liked to believe that's what made her strong. Sam knew she didn't need anyone to lean on, especially not a man. Actually, she was a bit thankful her father had made her stand on her own two feet. She shuddered at the thought of being one of those clingy women.

But a little flirtation—and maybe more—

with Brady Stone seemed to be rejuvenating her depressed state. Seeing him just a few stolen moments here and there helped her hectic days pass with much more pleasure.

When her eyes started to burn from glaring at a computer screen for too long, Sam glanced to the corner of the monitor.

Oh, God. It was 5:59.

She quickly saved the proposal she'd been working on and turned her computer off. She took a swig from the tepid bottle of water on her desk and turned off her lights.

After racing down the hall to the elevator and getting on, she sagged in relief against the cool metal.

But then stiffened as she caught her reflection in the steel doors.

Oh, this was not good. How could she

continue her flirtatious, so-far-harmless fling with Brady if she looked like she'd pressed her suit with a crimping iron?

Strands of hair tangled around her shoulders. Her makeup had worn off, her concealer giving way to her dark circles. She not only looked rumpled, she had the appearance of a haggard raccoon.

Oh, yeah, she was looking good.

The elevator dinged on the top floor. Sam took a deep, calming breath and stepped out, fully intent on backing out of the dinner date.

She knocked on his suite door and waited. But when the door flew open with a smiling Brady standing on the other side, her recently rehearsed speech fled her mind.

Five

"I thought you'd gotten a better offer," he said as he motioned her in.

"Not a better offer, but I do have to cancel." She remained in the hallway, trying not to look beyond the alluring man to the candlelit dinner by the French doors. "I ran later with work than I intended and I'm a mess. Perhaps we can do this another time? Say when I have time to freshen up?"

He reached for her hand, pulled her inside. "Nonsense, you're here now and you look beautiful as always."

Sam allowed herself to be drawn into the lion's den.

Why did she feel like prey for this over-powering man? And why did she let him persuade her decisions?

Because she liked being needed, even if only for a while. And because she was a woman. A woman who found herself a little too attracted to a total stranger. So what if her appearance wasn't perfect? Obviously, he didn't care, which just proved yet another point—Brady Stone obviously wanted to be near her for no other reason than because he enjoyed being with her as she did him.

A mixture of enticing aromas filled her

senses. Between the scrumptious-smelling dinner and Brady's fresh, masculine scent, her reasons for leaving fled her mind.

Sam's gaze traveled across the suite, through the patio doors where the sun still remained high in the sky. A small, intimate glass table with one tapered candle and two plates covered with silver domes beckoned her closer.

"Looks like you've thought of everything." She crossed the plush beige carpeting. Being alone with Brady in such a personal atmosphere made her nerves jitter with excitement, her heart pound with anticipation. "I hope you didn't go to any trouble."

"None at all," he assured in that rich, deep tone that gave her chills.

A delicate pink rose lay beside one of the

table settings. Twice in just over twenty-four hours this amazing man had brightened her dull days with a touch of beauty.

"This looks lovely," she told him, turning around.

He smiled, taking one long stride after another until he came within a foot of her. "It goes with the company."

Why did such come-on lines work so well when they came from his mouth? No grown woman with any sense would fall for this smooth-talking charmer. Obviously, where this man was concerned all her judgment flew out the window. And for some unknown reason, she didn't care.

"I don't know how good my company will be." She looked up into his dark eyes, breathed in his hypnotizing scent and trudged on with her plan to get out of his presence. "I haven't stopped since this morning and I'm afraid if I sit, I may fall asleep in my plate. So, you see, not good company."

His eyes darted to her lips. "Then I'll have to do something to keep you awake."

Before she could even take a breath, he stepped closer, his mouth claimed hers.

The shock only lasted a moment before pure pleasure took control. Brady's arms wrapped around her waist, pulling her taut against his hard, lean body.

She had no choice but to answer his demand with one all her own. She didn't want to take the time to consider how much time had passed since she'd been held this way, kissed this way. Nor did she want to acknowledge the fact she needed the intimacy more than her next breath. And she certainly didn't want to think about how fast Brady was moving. So what if she'd only known him two days?

His tongue parted her lips. She let him in.

She slid her arms around his neck, threading her fingers through his thick, wavy hair. No way would she let him ease back, not now that she'd tasted him.

Brady's hands splayed across her back, his fingertips dug into her suit jacket, creating an arousing friction from the warmth of his hand and the satin material on her bare skin.

A moan escaped. Hers, his? She didn't

know. Did it matter since their mouths were fused as one?

He nipped at her bottom lip. "I've been dying to do that for two days."

Breathless, Sam opened her eyes. "I'm glad you didn't wait any longer."

"I don't normally attack women, but I can't control myself around you."

"Attack? If only I'd get attacked like that more often, maybe I wouldn't be so caught up in work."

His soft chuckle vibrated through his chest and against hers. "Are you awake now?"

"Huh?"

"You said you were tired."

Disappointment flooded through her. She unlaced her hands, releasing her hold on him and stepped back. "Oh, um, yes."

"Now, don't get your back all up again."

"I don't know what you're talking about," she said, even though she'd knowingly tilted her chin and straightened her shoulders.

He closed the short gap she'd created. "I was just using your tiredness as my excuse."

Sam placed a hand on his chest before he could lean down again. "You don't strike me as the kind of man who needs an excuse to kiss a woman. Especially if you always kiss with such…passion."

Brady's enticing smile widened. "Passion? Does that mean you'll stay awake and keep me company?"

His scorching stare roamed over her face, doing nothing to squelch the desire that had erupted inside her.

Perhaps dinner was a mistake. How could

she concentrate on anything else other than the desire to get completely naked with this man she'd known for only forty-eight hours?

His heart beat in a calm, easy manner beneath her palm. Obviously he wasn't as worked up as she.

Did she affect him in any way whatsoever? Was his attention toward her typical as with any other woman? There wasn't a shred of doubt in her mind that Brady had more experience in the sexual department than she.

"Look," she said, removing her hand from his chest, distancing herself from temptation. "I'm running a resort, so my time is pretty limited. I don't even know if I have time for a fling."

Brady's intense stare lasted only a second

before he erupted into laughter. "Do you always speak what's on your mind?"

"There's no misconception that way."

"I'm not into flings, either." His eyes darted back down to her lips. "I want to spend time with you while I'm here. Tonight we'll have dinner. No pressure."

Before she could answer, her cell vibrated in her pocket. "I have to take this," she said, pulling out her phone.

"Take your time. I'll pour us some wine."

He moved away, giving her the privacy she needed. Without bothering to glance at the caller ID, she flipped up her phone. "Hello."

"These numbers are unacceptable, Samantha."

Glasses clinked over her shoulder, but the

noise did nothing to drown out her father's anger. "What do you mean?"

"The number of guests is down ten percent this quarter. I trusted you to bring the numbers up."

Sam stepped farther away from Brady. "I'm doing what I can. If we could sit and talk about my ideas—"

"Not this again." Stanley grunted. "I just want you to do what I sent you to do. Don't second-guess me and don't forget who's in charge."

Sam jerked as if he'd slapped her. Thankfully, the love seat was nearby. She sank onto the cushions. "As if I could."

"Are you in your office?" he asked.

Sam's gaze darted to Brady. "I had to step out for a moment."

Stanley let out a sigh. "Perhaps you should concentrate on your work instead of socializing, Samantha. My resort won't run itself."

Sam ended the call, suddenly not in the mood for dinner—or Brady. Her father always managed to toss cold water on anything good in her life. She found it sad the man did nothing but stew about business and finances.

No wonder her mother had been unhappy.

Brady's grip on the wine bottle tightened. He had a feeling his plans for the night had just evaporated. And for the first time in his life, business wasn't in the forefront of his mind.

The hurt and the confusion in Sam's eyes

had him placing the bottle on the table and crossing to her.

She glanced up when he brushed a strand of hair off her shoulder. "Are you okay?" he asked.

Pushing to her feet, she stood, her body brushing his. "Just business." She pasted on a fake smile. "But I'm afraid I won't be very good company tonight. Could we do this another time?"

Because he knew she didn't want to appear weak, especially in front of a virtual stranger, he nodded. "Absolutely."

She hadn't said who was on the other end of the call, but Brady knew. Speaking with Stanley Donovan was obviously upsetting to everyone.

He escorted Samantha to the door, all

the while cursing her father. Besides the fact Brady needed to get information from Sam, he'd planned on doing a little seducing, as well.

But more than that, he hated the fact the old man could wipe the light right out of Sam's eyes in a matter of moments.

He couldn't afford to let her innocence and vulnerability get to him. Business was business. He had to keep telling himself that or he'd be pulled under by Samantha's sweet way.

She turned to him once they reached the door.

"Thanks for going to all the trouble."

Without another word, she opened the door and left.

Brady turned only to have the cozy table

by the patio doors mock him. This was not how he'd planned the evening. Granted he'd planned a little seduction and a little deceiving, but he certainly hadn't wanted Sam to leave hurt and confused.

With a tightening in his chest, Brady moved to the desk, picked up his phone and dialed Cade.

"Hello."

"We have a problem."

"What's wrong?"

Brady walked back to the sitting area, taking the warm seat Sam had just vacated. "Stanley just called Sam and, from the one-sided conversation I overheard, he's mad about the report she sent."

Cade muttered a curse. "Did she say anything about the call?"

"She's too discreet to discuss business with me." Brady rested his elbows on his knees and rubbed his forehead. "My concern now is Stanley finding out about my stay here. I need to step up my game plan."

"Sounds to me like he's just as much of a jerk to his own daughter as he is to everyone else."

Brady had gotten that impression, as well. How could a father be so harsh to his own child? How could *any* man treat Sam with such disrespect?

God, he was no better than her father. Disrespect? Brady had disrespected Sam from the moment she'd walked up to the registration desk to assist him. Backing down now, though, was not an option he would even entertain. Sam would get caught in the crossfire, but there wasn't a thing he could do about it. Business always came first. Period.

Besides, he owed this mission to his father. This property had been purchased and the first shovel of dirt dug by his dad when Brady had been only ten years old. The name Lani Kaimana was chosen by his mother. She'd always wanted to live in Kauai and his father had made sure she always had a place to come to. Lani Kaimana had been his family's first resort, and Brady needed to bring ownership back to its rightful place. So Sam's feelings, and his for that matter, could not interfere with his conquest.

"What do you want me to do?" Cade asked.

"Nothing. I just wanted to give you heads-up

in case Donovan decides to make a move on another property."

"Keep me posted."

"Same here," Brady said. "Talk to you later."

As he disconnected the call, Brady knew he should find Sam and make sure she was truly okay. But first, he'd let her have some privacy.

He hated that he had to use her feelings to his advantage, but he had no choice—not if he wanted to ruin Stanley Donovan. Brady had never let his hormones control a business transaction and he didn't intend to start now.

Brady pocketed his key card and left his suite. He had no clue what room Sam occupied here, or even if she stayed on the grounds. All he knew was he needed to find her.

He'd start with her office and go from there. Once he made sure she was okay, he could return to his original agenda.

<u>Six</u>

Two days. Two whole days had passed since he'd seen Sam—not for lack of trying to find her. Obviously she was busy and didn't want to be found, but Brady wasn't giving up. He had to get Sam, get closer to her.

He made his way down the wide marble hall for the umpteenth time in the past forty-eight hours.

She had to return to her office sometime.

Clearly she was a hard worker and not someone to sit behind her desk all day and delegate orders.

Surprisingly, her office door was ajar. He peeked his head inside, expecting to find Sam at her desk nursing another migraine. But her office was empty.

Being a man to take advantage of every opportunity, he stepped inside the spacious room and took a seat at her desk. He hadn't planned on glancing at the paperwork lying on top of the desk calendar, but, well, it was there and he couldn't resist.

His eyes roamed over the budget proposal, his mind agreeing with each number he saw. Not only that, Brady found himself intrigued by the renovation ideas she'd listed at the bottom. This woman had smart business sense—unlike her father. Perhaps business was her forte after all. His respect for her kicked up a notch.

With ideas like the ones listed on the paper, Lani Kaimana could be the most prestigious resort in the world. The ideas had to be Sam's. Stanley couldn't come up with something this good, this fresh and new.

If old man Donovan listened to Sam, this resort would be absolutely packed. Brady only wished he had someone as talented and passionate about her work in his corner.

A brilliant idea popped into his head and he nearly jumped out of his seat with excitement.

He needed to get Samantha Donovan on his team.

But first, he had to gain back the resort.

God, if all his plans fell into place—and in the order he intended—not only would he have his property back, he'd have Samantha as a major asset to his company.

"Looking for something?"

Brady jerked, his gaze locking with Sam's. The muscle in her jaw clenched as she stood leaning against her doorway, arms crossed over her chest. He'd been so absorbed in her proposal, he hadn't heard her come in.

Brady cleared his throat. "You."

She made her way toward her desk, coming to stand beside him. "If you're done snooping through my business, I have work to do."

In no hurry to leave, Brady leaned back in the creaky, leather chair. "I won't use much of your time. First of all I wanted to make sure you were all right. I was worried the other night."

"I'm fine. Thank you."

"Good. Second—" he pointed to her paperwork "—that's some pretty impressive stuff. Are you planning on a major overhaul of this resort?"

Sam let out a short, clipped laugh. "If I had my say."

He came to his feet, ready to lay his own proposal on the line. "So, those plans aren't set into motion?"

"I wish."

"What I saw impressed me," he told her, trying to smooth out his path.

He couldn't have her doubting his trust and presence now. He'd come too far and had too much to lose.

"Really?" Her tone softened as she leaned a hip against the desk. "Why is that?"

"I own a real estate company with my brother and we specialize in renovating resorts and businesses. You really know what you're talking about here."

Her eyes darted to the open file. "Thank you."

"I'm serious," he reiterated. "You've got good business sense."

"I appreciate that, even though you were snooping."

She placed a hand on the desk and leaned her body onto it, drawing his attention to her simple, white button-up shirt as it drew across her breasts. Her attention, however, was on the file.

He redirected his attention. "Your figures are impressive."

Sam's mouth quirked up as her eyes darted to his. "I know what you think of my figure. Now, I have to get back to work if you're done chatting about useless ideas."

Brady resisted the urge to kiss her again. "First of all, I meant the figures here." He pointed down to the file he'd been caught reading. "Second, these are hardly useless."

"My father disagrees."

Brady placed his hands on her shoulders. "Then we'll make him understand."

Samantha's brows drew together. "I barely know you. Why would you offer such a thing?"

"Listen to me before you make up your

mind." His heart beat so fast he feared she'd hear the thumping. "This resort has more potential, and from the look of your proposal, you know it, too. I have properties I'm acquiring that I could use input on from someone with such verve for renovating."

Her eyes roamed over his face. "I appreciate your enthusiasm in my work, but I still don't understand why you'd want to do this. Aren't you here to work yourself?"

Her unsureness didn't faze him. He had an agenda and he would see it through.

"I overheard your conversation with your father," Brady told her. "I know he doesn't appreciate you or your ideas. I see what you have to offer and it shouldn't be wasted."

She shook her head and glanced away.

"This isn't a good idea. Now, if you'll excuse me, I have to get back to work."

Brady nodded and exited her office. He'd let her chew on the suggestion he'd planted in her head and see how she felt once she calmed down.

And once he let Cade in on his plan, there would be no way Sam could refuse the two Stone boys.

Sam studied her proposal, warmed at the thought someone took her seriously. But she wasn't giving up on her father. If she gave up on her dream for this resort, she'd regret it.

Just like she regretted ever talking to Brady Stone. He'd planted an idea in her head and she wished she could erase the tempting thought from her memory.

Could she trust a virtual stranger to help her rejuvenate this resort? Heaven knows he'd done wonders in reviving her once-buried sexual urges.

But this was business, and she had to keep her personal emotions locked away.

Running this resort was her one—and probably only—chance to prove herself to her father. If, and that was a big *if,* she let Brady in and confided in him, what would stop him from using her weakness to open a greater resort right next door? Kauai was a growing island and the last thing she needed was another competitor.

Sam laughed. Obviously her father's cynicism had rubbed off on her. Her gut told her to trust Brady. Besides, at this point, she needed someone in her corner.

Sam took a seat at her desk, picked up her phone and dialed her brother's office line. His secretary put the call through immediately.

"Sam." Miles's low, silky voice came through the phone. "What's up?"

"Has Dad talked to you about the resort?" she asked.

"I know he's upset."

Miles paused, just enough to arouse Sam's curiosity. "About?"

"Ask Dad."

Sam eased back in her seat, tucking the phone between her shoulder and her ear. "I'm asking *you*."

He sighed. "It's not my place to say."

Frustration flooded through her. "The more you and Dad keep me out of the loop, the more damage you're doing to the company.

Communication is the key to running a good business."

Miles laughed. "Sounds like you need to take your argument to the top, little sister."

"I'm an equal here," she told him. "I need to know what's going on that you're not telling me."

"All right. Dad is concerned that if the numbers don't go up he'll have to bring someone else in as manager or, as a last resort, he'll have to sell. He's giving you six more months."

Shock and disbelief settled into her chest. "What?"

"Now you see why Dad was so insistent on you turning the place around," Miles explained.

"How could the two of you keep something

this vital from me?" she demanded, gripping the phone.

"It wasn't my idea."

Without saying goodbye, Sam hung up on her brother, more upset now than she'd been before.

With her blood pressure rising, she punched in the number to her father's office. He answered on the second ring.

"Samantha, I'm very busy. Can this wait?"

Obviously he'd looked at his caller ID, so why did he even answer?

"No, it can't." For once he would listen to her, and she would come before his precious company.

"Make it fast."

Sam crossed her legs, rocked back in her

leather chair. "Why the hell wasn't I informed that I've been working on a probationary period?"

"I didn't feel it necessary to inform you."

Sam gripped her padded armrest. "Miles knows."

Her father sighed. "Sam, let it drop. You just take care of my resort."

Blood pulsed through her head. Her teeth clenched.

"Fine," she told him. "I'll take care of everything on my end."

Once she'd hung up the phone, Sam forced herself to breathe in slowly and exhale the same way. She needed to calm down and think before making any rash decisions.

She'd tried. Nearly all her life she'd tried to gain her father's respect. As an adult she'd practically begged him to earn a place in his company. Now she saw what he was really doing. As if she were a child, he seemed to just pat her on the head and humor her, giving her small jobs to keep her out of his hair—and even that was temporary.

Well, no more. She was more than ready to be appreciated, more than ready to be taken seriously as a businesswoman.

She wasn't sure what step to take next, but she knew one thing, she was done being pushed around by her father and her brother. Controlling men were officially a thing of her past. From here on out if they didn't see her for the talented career woman she'd become, she would do what she wanted, what was best for her. Risky decisions may come back to haunt her, but she had to do something drastic—or at least consider her options.

And if her father and Miles didn't appreciate her, she knew of someone who would make them.

Seven

Brady had just folded his last pair of khakis and placed them in his suitcase when someone knocked on his suite door.

Who could that be? He hadn't called down for the bellboy yet.

He opened his door and smiled at Sam.

She clasped her hands together. "I'd like to talk, if you have a minute."

He motioned her in. "Please."

She stepped in, bringing her soft, jasmine scent with her. Brady inhaled one good, deep breath. Enough to fill his lungs with the sweet aroma of Sam and just enough to entice him even more.

He closed the door and turned. "Is something wrong?"

"Depends."

Sam's gaze darted about, her teeth worried her bottom lip. She was nervous about something, and he should be glad. But instead he was concerned.

He gestured toward the sofa. "Have a seat."

Sam glanced across the room toward the bed, noticing the almost-packed suitcase. "Are you leaving?"

"I need to get back to the office for a

meeting with my attorney. I was hoping to see you before I left."

She took a seat on the couch and crossed her elegant, bare legs, allowing her pale blue skirt to inch up just that much more on her tan thigh. Brady swallowed hard and resisted the urge to adjust in his seat.

"Well, then, I'm glad I caught you before you left." She rested her elbow on the arm of the sofa, clasped her hands together and tilted her chin. "I've been thinking about your proposition."

Did he dare hope she'd reconsidered?

"But first I want to know if you were serious when you said you saw more potential with this resort, because this place means everything to me."

He knew the feeling. Lani Kaimana *was*

his family. It was the backbone of his father's legacy and the foundation they'd used to build upon. The Stone's literally *made* this place, and he would not see his bitter enemy destroy it over bad business decisions.

From this angle of attack, using Sam and her ideas, he could not only have the resort updated, but he'd be doing it all at the cost of Stanley Donovan.

Priceless. Absolutely priceless.

Her questioning eyes held his gaze, so he answered honestly. "Absolutely. I never lie about business."

She cleared her throat. "In that case, I'd like to discuss working with you on some plans. That is, if you'd planned on coming back."

Brady couldn't stop his mouth from

dropping open. He'd never guessed she'd actually come to him. Oh, sure, he'd hoped, but what made her change her mind in such a short amount of time?

"May I ask why the sudden change?" Now he did shift closer to the edge of his seat—every fiber of his being was aroused. "Last we talked you weren't even considering the notion."

"Let's just say I had a rude awakening. I'm not committing to anything, but I'd like to discuss how you intend to help me."

Oh, he intended to help her. He had to stay in control of this situation and use it to the advantage of his company.

The thrill of being one step closer to destroying the Donovans rushed through him. He reached out, brushed her hair from her shoulder. "Perhaps when I get back we can have dinner and discuss my plans."

"A business date?" she asked.

"We'll start there."

With a laugh, she came to her feet. "I don't think that's a good idea. Perhaps my coming here was a mistake."

Brady stood, as well, and, just as Sam turned, grabbed her arm. He couldn't let her leave, not when he was so close to getting what he wanted—and he wanted her. In his business. In his bed.

Her eyes met his, and he couldn't ignore the spark of desire. It practically radiated from her baby blues, from the heat in her body beneath his touch. This woman wasn't getting away so easily.

"Nothing about you being here with me is a mistake," he whispered. "Nothing."

Common sense went straight to hell as he lowered his mouth to hers, all the while keeping his gaze locked. He waited for a sign, something to make him stop. But when she parted her lips and fluttered her lids, he knew he'd received a sign…just not the one he'd expected.

His lips touched hers and a flood of emotions took over. Desire, passion, want. Need.

The sweetness she offered with only her mouth made his knees weak.

He'd never gotten weak knees over a woman before.

Opening her lips, she welcomed him in. His tongue swept through and, other than his hand on her upper arm, they remained apart.

But, God, he wanted to grab her and drag her down to the sofa. How easy this would be to have her clothes off and satisfied.

He knew she wanted this as much as he did, so why wasn't he taking what he'd wanted since he met her?

Because a woman like Samantha should be handled with care. Obviously something she wasn't used to. He intended to show her a different side of himself—one she wouldn't expect. One that would be impossible to dismiss.

Seduction was key in reaching his goal. He could tell Sam was the type who pretended not to need anyone, but deep down, she wanted the affection, the love.

Brady kissed the corners of her mouth and eased back.

"That's why we would have a hard time working together on this," she murmured, lifting her lids.

Her swollen mouth only looked more inviting, especially now that he'd tasted her again. "Because we can't contain our attraction?"

She nodded, her eyes darting back to his lips.

He stroked his thumb along her arm. "I don't see why we can't keep business separate from pleasure."

"What happens when we decide we've had enough of each other?" she asked. "Does your offer to help cease?"

Enough of each other? Since he hadn't had

her yet, he couldn't imagine getting enough of the lovely Sam Donovan.

"You make it sound as if we're already sleeping together."

She shrugged. "Are you saying we wouldn't if we continued to see each other on any level?"

Brady swallowed the lump in his throat. "You do really speak your mind, don't you?"

"Are we or aren't we sexually attracted to each other?"

"We are."

Her heavy-lidded eyes roamed over his face. "I assumed sex is what you wanted from me."

Why did that sentence sound so, so…dirty? Even though he did want to sleep with her, why did he feel like he was cheating her, and himself, of something more?

"I won't lie. The thought of you naked in my bed is more than appealing."

She smiled. "This is all moving a bit fast for me. I mean, I didn't even know you a few days ago and now you want me to trust you with my business and my body. I keep asking myself what you'll get out of all this."

Brady wasn't surprised at her hesitation. This was a woman who would make a man beg and not even realize he's doing it. Damn if he didn't wish they'd met under different circumstances.

He couldn't very well tell her what he'd get out of this appealing offer.

"What I'll get is the satisfaction of helping a woman I've come to admire gain her equal footing in her father's company." He stroked her shoulders. "I know how hard this industry is. Besides, I'll get a side benefit of seeing you, touching you."

She shivered beneath his touch and Brady refused to let the guilt creep up. He reassured her with a soft kiss to her lips before drawing away. He had to maintain some distance every now and then to keep his own emotions from getting boggled up in this mess.

"I do have to get back to my office," he told her. "I'll be returning to the island in a week or so. I plan on purchasing a vacation home in the area and I want to keep my eye on it."

Samantha nodded. "I can't wait to get started on the resort proposal."

"And my personal proposal?"

She lifted one perfectly arched brow. "I'll let you know."

Flying several thousand feet above the Pacific Ocean in his private jet, Brady turned off his cell. He didn't feel like chatting with Cade anymore about Lani Kaimana or Sam—*especially* Sam.

Brady had called Cade when he'd first boarded his jet and explained the progress he'd made, but his brother zeroed in on Sam, claiming Brady was getting in too deep with her.

Cade didn't understand. Hell, Brady didn't understand himself what was going on with his emotions. But he did know he had to keep trudging on with this plan.

Sam would get hurt, that was a fact. But would he? Doubtful. If he had the resort back how could he be remorseful?

Perhaps Sam had gotten under his skin, but so what? Obviously, from the way she'd kissed him last night, he'd gotten under hers, as well. He just had to stay there.

Their sexual chemistry would just make his plan flow that much smoother. He intended to not only get Samantha Donovan in his bed, but gain back his lost property. There was no reason in the world he couldn't have both.

As far as he was concerned, she didn't need to find out who he was, and thankfully most of the staff had been replaced since his father's ownership, so he wasn't recognized.

Brady watched the pillowy white clouds

pass beneath him as he settled deeper into his leather sofa. Samantha was definitely a perk he hadn't expected, but one he would thoroughly enjoy.

She wouldn't deny him. He'd seen the look of desire and passion in her eyes, felt it in her kiss. She was a woman and women had needs just like men. He intended to meet her needs until he got what he wanted.

His list of wants was simple: Samantha in his bed, his resort back and Stanley Donovan's empire obliterated.

When he returned to Kauai, he wouldn't leave again without each item on the list checked off.

Eight

"The old conference room needs to be cleared out." Sam nestled the phone between her ear and shoulder as she typed up her budget plan for the new day care center. "I want that whole area emptied because we're turning it into a day care for parents who want some alone time."

"Are you sure, Ms. Donovan?" the head maintenance man asked. "This is the first I've heard about this."

Sam resisted the urge to sigh as she went on. "I'm sure, Phillip. The conference room hasn't been used for as long as I've been here and nothing is scheduled. We still have the ballroom for receptions, so if need be, we can hold meetings in there. Now, please, clear out the room and let me know when the job is done so I can get a construction crew in there to build some dividers."

"You're the boss."

Yeah, she was. If only her father would see that.

Samantha reviewed her notes and saved the file. No, the day care hadn't been approved by her father, but if she wanted to get ahead in his company, and gain his approval, she had to take initiative. Now parents could take at least a few hours to themselves, maybe have a nice lunch or a romantic walk on the beach.

Romantic walk. On. The. Beach.

No matter what she did, her thoughts always drifted back to Brady Stone and his ridiculously affecting charm. She'd never been one to fall for smooth talkers before.

Physically, Brady had left, but the potent man still lingered in her mind, in her office where he'd had dinner for her and along the beach every time she glanced out the window.

Damn. She wished she had more willpower where he was concerned, but she was a woman and he was an extremely sexy man who, for some insane reason, found her attractive and actually wanted to help her. How could she even try to resist?

Samantha shook her head, hoping to clear all the Brady thoughts from her mind, and came to her feet. She needed to get out of her office and make sure all was running smoothly in her—*her*—hotel. After all, this resort was her baby, and she intended to spoil it.

Even though she and Brady were going to work on this together, she planned on getting a jump start before he returned. Hopefully her days would go by more quickly and she could fill the void he'd left.

"Abby, hold my calls, I need to talk to Brady."

Brady led the way up to his second-floor office.

"What's up?" Cade asked, closing the office door behind him.

Brady took a seat behind his desk and rested his elbows on the glossy mahogany top. "I'm going back to the resort in a few days."

Cade nodded, resting his hands on the back of the leather wingback chair opposite the desk. "Has she given you any ammo we can use against her old man?"

"None, yet. But I have a feeling with a few more one-on-one occasions, it's just a matter of time before I can really pump her for information."

"Just be careful," Cade warned. "She'll discover who you are eventually."

He hoped like hell she didn't. "I'll have the information we need to destroy the Donovans beforehand. Trust me," Brady said. "I'll get what we need. I just want you to be aware that I may be on the island for a while. I don't intend to come back until the job is done."

Cade shook his head with a laugh. "An exotic island, a beautiful woman—albeit the enemy—and a plan of seduction. Man, you get all the cushy, rewarding jobs."

Brady grinned, resting back in his seat. "Just part of being the oldest."

"Just make sure you get this done right. We don't want to let Dad down."

Brady held his brother's stare. No, they wouldn't let their father down. And that was all the reason Brady needed not to fall under Sam's spell.

"What the hell is this I hear about a day care?"

Samantha held the phone away from her

ear as her father's booming voice punctured her eardrum.

She should've known she'd be ratted on. Was she in a corporation or junior high?

"Who told you?"

"It doesn't matter," he scolded. "Maybe you forgot our numerous conversations where I not only didn't authorize this preposterous plan, I flat-out denied your request."

"Yes, I remember," she agreed like going against the great Stanley Donovan was no big deal. "But I am the manager and I see what's going on here and what the patrons want. Many couples would like some private time to enjoy the tranquility of the island without kids running around and screaming at them. Surely that's something you could relate to."

That last sentence slipped out of her mouth before she could think, but once the words were out, she didn't regret them. Stanley Donovan had never been a hands-on father. Quite the opposite. Before the death of Sam's mother, Bev Donovan had done it all. After her death, well, Stanley paid nannies and eventually shipped his daughter off to boarding school in Switzerland.

"As of this moment, you will be checking in with me at the beginning and end of each business day."

Sam slammed her fist into her desk. "What? You can't be serious."

"I'm dead serious. If you can't follow my directions, you will have to report every day and let me know what your plans are. I want to know everything from the number of guests to the number of rolls of toilet paper in the storage room."

Rage filled her. "This is not how you treat Miles."

"Miles doesn't go behind my back."

Samantha gripped the phone. "Fine. You'll get your daily report, but don't blame me when your resort fails because you were too bullheaded to see some changes need to be made."

"Your attitude needs some major adjusting, little girl, or you'll find yourself out of a job."

"I bust my butt around here and have never been given any praise, much less a thank-you. You have no idea what I do."

"Things that I don't agree with," he interjected.

"I won't let this resort go belly-up. You seem to not care about it, but I do."

Slamming the phone down, Samantha gained a slight bit of satisfaction in the fact that her father was still talking. She'd really just about had it. She'd never been treated like a problem employee and she'd certainly never hung up on her boss, but she'd never worked for her father before.

Her hands shook from all the anger pumping through her. She counted to five, then ten, and even when she got to twenty, she was still enraged.

How dare he speak to her as if she were a child? He didn't take the time to discipline her when she'd been young, why would he start now?

Sam shoved back from her desk and stood.

She needed to take a walk, cool off and then resume her duties that would continue to go unappreciated.

She flung open her door and slammed directly into a wall of solid muscle and sexy man.

"Whoa." Brady grabbed hold of her arms. "What's the hurry?"

She stared up at him. "What are you doing back?"

His soft chuckle penetrated the wall of anger she'd erected. "I told you I'd be back."

"But you only left three days ago. You said a week."

He shrugged. "I got done earlier than expected. Besides, I missed you."

Those three simple words melted her, made her knees weaken.

How could he have known just what she needed and how on earth did he know she was having a really, really bad day? For anyone else, she would've made an excuse to be alone but with Brady, well, she wanted his company.

She reached up, wrapped her fingers around his wrists. "Can we talk?"

"Of course."

With his hold still on her arms, he backed her into her office, shut the door with his foot and captured her mouth.

On a sigh, she molded into him. Like a starving woman, she took everything he offered as she slid her hands up his arms and curled her fingers around his strong, muscular shoulders. His wide hands slid around her waist and drew her closer…as if she'd go anywhere now. She tasted his need, his desire and she was almost certain he could taste hers, as well.

Heat pooled between her legs, her nipples pressed achingly against her silky bra. The need for this man gave her no choice but to respond to his arousing kiss.

If this man could make her damp with just a kiss, what would he do to her in bed?

<u>Nine</u>

Brady didn't relinquish his hold as he eased his mouth from hers. "I've been thinking about that for days. I knew you'd be worth the wait."

Confused, stunned and incredibly turned on, Sam opened her eyes and peered up at him. "I don't think we should be doing this."

"Why not?" His brows drew together.

Good question. She had to push aside her desire and longing to recall the excuse she'd rehearsed in her head.

"Because I don't move this fast," she said through her thick voice. "Not that I'm not incredibly attracted to you, but getting a quickie in my office isn't my idea of romantic or professional."

He studied her face, his thumbs still caressing her neck. "I appreciate your honesty, so I'll be truthful, as well. I want to lay you down on that desk and make you scream. Romantic or not, that's my fantasy."

Her nipples tightened at the erotic image. "Brady." She placed her hands on his hard chest, his pecs fitting perfectly in her palms. "Think about this. If we have sex—"

"*When* we have sex…"

Rolling her eyes, she laughed. "Let's just enjoy each other while you're here on business. If we get to know each other, and things progress at a natural, slower pace, that's fine. No expectations. Okay?"

His chocolate eyes turned serious. "Fair enough. But I should warn you, I won't stop trying to fulfill my fantasy."

God, when he spoke in that low, seductive tone she wanted to take him up on the desk offer. But she couldn't—not yet. Her career had to come first no matter how much she wanted Brady.

But just once in her life she wished she'd be a bad girl and put her personal needs first. Why did every fiber of her being have to be so damn good all the time?

* * *

After an hour of concentrating on breathing, Sam was able to get back to work. She honestly didn't know how much more willpower she had left. She liked to think she had quite a lot, but she feared if Brady kissed her again, she wouldn't even be able to define the word *willpower.*

Brady told her he'd be busy with conference calls the rest of the afternoon, but he'd like to see her tonight if she had the time.

On one hand she appreciated the space he offered, but on the other, she wished he'd tell her he couldn't wait another minute to strip her down and get to know every inch of her body and to hell with business.

If he told her he couldn't wait to be with

her, that he wanted to spend the night, she'd cave with no regrets.

But he'd been a gentleman and told her he respected her decision. How could she be so tough with her willpower when he had her defensive walls crumbling?

Her cell rang just as she was about to pull up the upcoming-guest list for the following week.

She slipped the cell from her Prada jacket pocket. "Hello."

"Sam, are you busy?" Miles asked.

"No. Are you calling to scold me, as well?"

Samantha settled back in her seat. Getting a call from Miles was better than her father, but not much.

"Dad doesn't know I'm calling," he explained.

"Aren't you afraid you'll get grounded?" she joked.

"Will you be serious for a minute?"

She sighed. "Fine. What is so urgent that you had to go behind father's back and call the enemy?"

"You're not the enemy, Sam."

"Whatever." She waved a hand through the air. "The reason for this call is…"

"Dad is making some major changes and your little stunt didn't help. Things are getting chaotic around here, so if you could lay low and just do what you're told, that would really help."

Samantha snorted. "You're kidding, right? I'm doing double the work of anybody else in his company and receiving little to no recognition and you want me to lay low?"

"I take it you don't know about the changes?"

Sitting up in her seat, Sam feared she wouldn't like what she was about to hear. "Do you really think he'd tell me anything? Besides, he was too busy berating me."

Miles paused a little too long for her liking. "We've hired a new V.P. He will be taking my place and I will be taking Dad's place. Father plans on retiring soon."

Her heart sank. Obviously she hadn't been considered for this promotion. She was a Donovan, but not enough of one to be part of the family's major decision makers in the corporation.

"Did he even consider me for a higher position?" She almost hated to ask.

"No."

"This is unacceptable," Sam all but shouted. She didn't know if she wanted to punch something or cry.

After all she'd done for that company, how could they do this? Did they not have a caring bone in their bodies? She knew the answer, she just didn't want to face reality.

As usual, the Donovan empire reigned above all else. Even her feelings.

Obviously her father and Miles had had someone in mind for a while or the hiring process would've taken longer.

"Sam?"

"I've got to go."

She disconnected the call, and for the second time that day she needed some fresh air. Unfortunately, this time when she opened her door, Brady wasn't there to greet her with open arms and a mind-numbing, toe-curling kiss.

Samantha made her way through the lobby and onto the beach. She slid off her Gucci sandals and hooked the straps around her fingers.

Now that she'd had time to absorb Miles's bombshell, she realized she was beyond pissed, beyond hurt.

Samantha knew she wouldn't get any more work done today, so she decided to do what she always did when she was upset and wanted to take out frustrations on something. She went back to her room at the resort and cleaned.

Oh, there were plenty of maids, but

Samantha would rather have them cleaning up after an actual guest than herself. Besides, she didn't dirty too much considering most of her time was spent in her office or milling about the hotel making sure everyone was happy.

Sam threw on her sloppy clothes. She had no intention of going anywhere for a while.

With tattered exercise shorts and a white tank, she grabbed her bucket of cleaning supplies.

She scoured her bathtub until it was sparkling white. She searched for dust bunnies to attack and found only one. She reorganized her clothes in her closet and still, still wasn't satisfied with her self-cleansing.

She had, however, worked up a nice sweat. Just as she was about to make use of her freshly cleaned tub, someone pounded on her suite door.

Sam glanced down at herself and hoped it wasn't an employee needing to talk. She was not exactly in boss mode.

She glanced through the peephole and groaned. Be careful what you wish for.

With no other option than to be seen at her worst, Sam opened the door.

Brady's eyes raked over her. "Cleaning day?" he asked with a smile.

"Yeah. What are you doing here?"

He shrugged and stepped in. "I was hoping you'd take me up on the dinner I offered earlier."

He turned to face her, looking so GQ in his white T-shirt, dark jeans and black belt and sandals.

God, she had to look like a madwoman in his eyes. The hair she'd yanked into a ponytail had halfway fallen and her makeup surely had worn off by now.

"I wish you would've rang my room first," she told him.

"Had I called, you would've found some excuse not to see me."

Maybe. "I'm such a mess, Brady. I've scrubbed my tub and reorganized my closet. I'm really not at my best."

"You look cute to me." He kissed her forehead and strode into her small yet cozy living area as if they'd not just met a little over a week ago. "Go ahead and finish. I'll just watch some TV until you're done cleaning."

Defeated and a little pleased that she hadn't

scared him away by her appearance, Sam followed him. "I'll be right back."

He picked up the remote, clicked on the flat-screen television. "I'll be waiting."

Sam rushed into her bathroom and ran a tubful of scalding-hot water to relax her tight muscles. She made sure to shave and wash with her jasmine-scented body wash.

It may have been a quickie bath, but when a man like Brady showed up at your front door, you had to at least try to look feminine. Freshly shaven legs and some scented lotion would go a long way.

As she towel dried she wondered why her heart beat like a sixteen-year-old's. This was a man she'd shared multiple kisses with. A man she was starting to care about and she believed cared for her, too.

A man who'd made his intentions clear. He wanted her. Bad.

Brady wasn't known for his patience, but for Sam he would make an exception. No, for the fact he was going to take the resort out from under her, he'd make the exception.

He wanted information and he wanted it yesterday.

But most of all, after that passionate kiss in her office, he wanted his hands on her again. He needed to feel her against him, needed to hear her soft groans.

Unable to concentrate on any program, Brady turned off the TV and settled back onto the plush, floral sofa. Behind him Sam's soft footsteps padded from her bedroom, and he smiled. Already her jasmine scent filled

JULES BENNETT   169

the room, making him all the more eager to touch her.

"Nothing on TV?" she asked as she took a seat beside him.

"Nothing important."

She'd left her hair damp, making the golden blond seem more dark honey. Her face was pink and she'd thrown on a pair of white cotton shorts and a black tank. And he was pretty sure there was no bra considering her nipples were pressing against the cotton.

"I've had a really bad day, so if you want to dine with me, can we just do room service?"

"Room service is fine."

Actually, spending an intimate evening in her suite, on her playing field, was perfect. Being in her own atmosphere would make her more relaxed, more open to share. He hoped.

Because he couldn't go another moment without touching her, he placed a hand on her bare thigh. "What do you want?"

She swallowed, her gaze darted down to his lips. "Anything. I'm starving."

That made two of them.

"I didn't realize how much I missed seeing you until I was gone," he told her. And much to his surprise, he wasn't lying.

Her hands came up to frame his face, and he was completely lost. Her soft touch aroused him, her trust humbled him, and Brady knew—just knew—he was going to hell for sure.

Ten

Before he could say another word, she pulled him in, capturing his mouth.

Dear Lord, this woman knew what she wanted. Talk about a complete turn-on.

Her lips prodded his until he opened, allowing her tongue access. She tasted minty and cool as if she'd just brushed her teeth.

He ran his hands up her dainty, bare arms,

easing down the straps of her tank. With just the tips of his fingers, he glided over the smooth slopes of her breasts, pleased when she arched into him.

Dipping his hands inside the shirt, he grabbed her bare breasts. Sliding his thumbs over her nipples proved to be satisfying for both of them, as they let out dueling groans.

Her hands slid down to his shoulders where she held on tight. Brady wanted more. He left her mouth to trail open-mouth kisses down her neck, across her collarbone.

Sam let out a moan when he moved his mouth lower.

He plucked a nipple into his mouth. Just as Sam let out another groan, the suite phone rang, the piercing sound cutting through the heavy breathing.

"I have a machine," she panted.

After the third ring, the machine picked up and Sam's soothing voice filtered through the air, asking the caller to leave a message.

"Samantha—" Her father's voice boomed through the room, and she all but froze in his arms. "Call me immediately. I'd better hear from you within the hour."

Rage filled him, but he suppressed the urge to curse. Did the old man have to ruin *everything?*

Sam pulled back, adjusted her tank and glanced up at him. "I'm sorry. That's my father."

Brady had to smile, he couldn't let her know

he already knew the voice of the devil. "Go call him. It sounds urgent."

"Everything's urgent with him, except what's important."

She went into her room, closed the door and left Brady wondering what she meant. Stanley was definitely a bastard, but to his own daughter? He'd suspected so before, but he'd heard the gruffness, the irritation in the old man's voice.

A part of Brady felt sorry for Sam, but the other part of him knew he couldn't get emotionally involved. He had to gain back this resort for his own father's sake.

Lani Kaimana held a special place in his heart and he wouldn't let it go, no matter what blue-eyed beauty crossed his path.

But the way she'd melted into his touch

had him wondering what if. If they'd met in San Francisco at his office, would they have become lovers on their own without his driving force pulling them together?

Yeah. No way would he have let Samantha go without trying—at the very least—to date her.

But right now he had access to all the ammunition he needed to destroy Stanley Donovan. While "helping" Sam, he would have her permission to look into files no enemy should see.

After several minutes of waiting, Brady picked up the phone in the living room and ordered room service. Some strawberries, finger sandwiches, wine. He didn't want anything major and he wanted things he could feed to Sam.

He needed to get back to the seduction he had going before Sam's father interrupted their evening.

But when Sam exited her bedroom with her cell in hand and a look of defeat on her face, he knew his plans for the evening may have just headed south.

"Everything okay?" he asked, coming to his feet and guiding her to the sofa.

"Just personal business."

"Want to talk about it?"

She nestled her head in the crook of his arm. "My father just made some decisions that I'd hoped he'd reconsider. Obviously he doesn't care about others' feelings."

"I don't know what's going on, but if you want to talk…"

She smiled up at him. "Thanks. I'd rather not."

Of course not. That would've been too easy.

"How about a movie?" he suggested. "I ordered room service, and it should be here any minute."

"Bless you."

While they waited on room service, they agreed on an action flick and, much to Brady's surprise, she'd not only seen the movie but loved it.

Great, now they had something in common other than Lani Kaimana and sexual attraction. As if he needed yet another reason to have his defenses soften toward this woman.

When the food arrived, Brady took care of

tipping the waiter and moved the silver cart beside the couch.

"Do you have a blanket?" he asked.

Her brows drew together. "Are you suggesting a carpet picnic?"

"Do you mind?"

A beaming smile spread across her face. "I'll be right back."

They spread the thick, cream-colored comforter from her bed in front of the couch and took a seat with their food, wine and glasses.

While the movie rolled in the background, Brady hand-fed Sam strawberries and nearly groaned when her tongue darted out to lick the juice running down his hand.

"This was the best idea," she said.

"You're the one who wanted to stay in," he reminded her.

"True, but you ordered the food."

He grinned. "Maybe we're just a good team."

Once all the food was gone, the wine empty, Brady settled with his back against the couch. Sam came to rest between his legs, her back against his chest. He wrapped his arms around her and, more than his next breath, he wanted to rip off that thin tank so he could feel her skin on his.

But he had to take this at her pace. The pace that was damn near killing him.

By the end of the movie, Sam was asleep.

Sam awoke in her bed, in the dark. With Brady at her side. Alarmed, she sat up.

"What?" Brady jerked. "Are you okay?"

Her eyes focused in the dark as she glanced back to him. "Um...how did we get here?"

"You fell asleep," he told her in a husky, sleep-filled voice. "I carried you in here."

Sam glanced back to her nightstand and groaned. "It's nearly 3:00 a.m. I'm so sorry, Brady."

"Sorry for what?"

When she turned her head, their lips nearly connected. "For falling asleep on you."

His gaze dropped to her mouth. "Do I look upset?"

She licked her lips. "You look turned on."

"I am."

"Are you going to make love to me?"

"Yes."

She moved a hand up his T-shirt, over his

shoulder and threaded her fingers through his hair. "Good."

He reached out, circling her wrist with his strong hand as his mouth came crashing down on hers. Both eager, frantic, they came to their knees with their mouths still fused.

Hands were everywhere, tugging at shirts, pulling on waistbands. Sam didn't recall wanting a man with everything in her. Nor did she recall loving how a man kissed so much. And Brady Stone could make her forget the world existed with just one hot, steamy kiss.

When he eased back to remove her shirt completely, his eyes widened. "You have no clue how long I've wanted you."

"I have a good idea."

In no time at all their clothes were strewn

about and they moved down on the bed together as one. Bare skin to bare skin. Lips to lips. Chest to chest.

The feel of his solid erection against her heated skin only made her hunger for more.

Instead of coming together, Brady rained kisses over her face, her shoulders, her chest and on down her abdomen. Instinctively, her legs parted as he settled between them.

He rested his hands on her inner thighs, spreading her before he tasted her. Sam arched off the bed, grabbed hold of his hands with her own and groaned. His cool mouth made quite the contrast to her heated center.

With slow—agonizingly slow—kisses

he continued to devour her as she writhed against him.

Just when she thought she couldn't take the assault anymore without screaming, he eased back up her body. "You taste so sweet, Sam."

"Take me," she pleaded. "Don't make me wait."

She reached into her nightstand drawer and pulled out a condom. Brady took the foil wrapper and in no time had himself sheathed.

He moved over her, spreading her legs wide with his hard thighs.

She eased her knees up, allowing him total access. Sam held on to his taut shoulders as he entered her in one swift move. The burning quickly gave way to pleasure.

Brady stilled, then as if a dam had broken free, he started moving his hips. His head dipped down to take a nipple. The soft, moist suction of his mouth combined with the hard, frantic pace of his hips nearly drove Sam insane.

She couldn't keep her eyes open another minute. Her fingers tightened over his muscled skin as he pulled out and thrust back in. Over and over again.

Sam cried out. She saw the bursts of light behind her lids. Warmth spread through her as she wrapped her legs around his waist, tilting her own hips to feel more.

"Yes, yes."

Brady captured her cries with his mouth. His tongue mimicking their lovemaking.

Her inner muscles clenched, and Sam let out one long moan.

Tingling sensations sped throughout her body as the climax rolled through her. And just when she thought she couldn't take any more, Brady pumped in and out in fast, frantic motions. Finally, his body shuddered, his hands gripped her thighs. Sam held on as his body tightened with his release.

When the tremors ceased, he rubbed his palms over her belly, her breasts. "Are you okay?"

"Ask me again when I can catch my breath."

Brady chuckled as he eased off the bed. In the distance she heard him running water in the bathroom.

Her body was beyond tired, beyond

satisfied. The man knew just where and how to touch a woman. He wasn't a selfish lover; if anything he cared more about her needs than his own. Why had she put him off for so long?

He didn't hesitate to climb between the rumpled sheets with her once again. Wrapping his arm around her waist.

She rolled over, pressed her backside into his front and relished the fact that she was in Brady Stone's arms. They'd made love and she couldn't be more pleased with her life right now.

Except for the fact her brother and father were still trying to control her, Sam was doing well. And even though they'd all but cast her aside, she knew in the long run, she'd be better off if she got out of the company for good.

She didn't want to be involved with any-body who thought they knew what was best for her. She wanted to be on equal terms with the men in her life. So far, Brady had proven he thought her his equal. Perhaps she should reconsider his business proposal. But right now, business was the last thing she wanted to think about.

She couldn't berate herself for allowing her lack of self-control to interfere with business. So far, every time Sam had needed someone, Brady had been there. And now that she'd shared her body, she knew trusting him with the business of revamping the resort was the right decision.

If the man was half as thorough with

business as he was in bed, Sam was quite certain that she'd made the right choice in going against her father's wishes and partnering up with Brady.

In the end, her father may just thank her.

With Brady's soft, warm breath on her neck, Sam drifted off to sleep, thankful she'd finally given in to her desires.

Eleven

"Sometimes I wonder what would've happened if my mother had lived."

Sam's soft voice drifted through the darkened room. Her back nestled into Brady's chest and he knew this intimate moment was about to get even more so. His heart was softening toward her even though he'd tried to steel himself.

Even so, he still had an agenda. Sam

couldn't, wouldn't, get in the way of his take-over plan. He knew, though, he wouldn't be able to keep his feelings for Sam out of this mess. He'd tried. Dammit, he'd tried, but Sam was a stronger force than he could handle.

He couldn't think about that now. Right now, he had to ignore the jab of guilt and keep trudging along with his plan of demise for the Donovans.

Moonlight flooded her spacious bedroom. All was quiet. No cell phones, no e-mails, no meetings. Right now, nothing existed but Sam.

"I often wonder the same thing about my mother," he confessed. He'd never, ever discussed his family with a woman. Especially in bed.

"It's hard growing up without them, isn't it?" she asked.

He swallowed the lump in his throat. "Yeah."

"I like to think she'd be proud of me."

Brady smiled in the darkness. "I didn't know your mother, but I'm sure she would've been."

"How do you know?"

He ran a finger down her side, dipping in at her waist and back out at her hip. "Because I know the woman you've become and I have to believe all the good in you stems from her. I have no doubt your mother is looking down on you with a smile on her face."

Sam turned in his arms. "I hope so. I only had her for a short time, but I miss her every day."

Because she was opening up, Brady kept the focus on her instead of talking about his own loss, reliving the nightmare. "Can you tell me about her?"

"She was beautiful." Sam's eyes misted, though a faint smile adorned her lips. "I remember her long blond hair. I loved brushing it and wishing my hair would be like that someday. She had a rich smile that would light up any room. And she cared. She truly cared about people and tried to put others' needs ahead of her own."

Brady tucked a stray tendril behind her ear. "Sounds like someone else I know."

Bright blue eyes came up. "I've been told we look exactly alike. My father used to tell me how beautiful she was."

He didn't want her happy memories

destroyed by thoughts of her father. "Go on about your mother."

"She stayed at home to care for me and Miles while my father worked." She laughed. "My father was always at work. The only time I saw him was when we'd have parties for his colleagues or around the holidays. Mom always made sure we never wanted for anything, and we didn't. At least, I didn't. Since Miles is older than me, Dad would take him to the office sometimes, but I stayed home with Mom. Occasionally, she'd go into the office and help him with some paperwork, but for the most part, she stayed home.

"We'd make cookies or watch a movie. Sometimes she'd take me shopping. When

I showed interest in dancing, she signed me up for dance classes."

Silence filled the room. Brady didn't coax her. He knew discussing this was hard for her. After all, he'd lost his mother when he was eleven and his own father only six months ago.

"One day we were running late for my class, and she was speeding," Sam said softly. "The weather was beautiful. The sun was shining and I was so happy because we were going to go get a puppy after my class. I was going to name him Baxter. But we never made it."

Brady continued his journey over her silky skin, hoping to relax her. "You don't have to tell me."

A tear escaped, sliding down to her hairline. "A car pulled out in front of us," she continued on as if she hadn't heard him. "I just remember my mother screaming then the sound of metal against metal. I was in the back, but I can still see the look in my mother's eyes in the rearview mirror just before we hit the other car."

Brady's heart ached for Sam. As she struggled to form words, he stroked her bare shoulder.

"She didn't die until we reached the hospital. There was internal bleeding," Sam explained with a sniff. "I only had a few minor injuries. Cuts, bruises, a broken collarbone from where I jerked against the seat belt. I overheard the doctors say I was lucky to be in the backseat."

"But you didn't feel lucky." It wasn't a question. Brady knew both the little girl and the woman sitting beside him had survivor's guilt.

"No," she whispered. "Why did she have to leave me? I needed her. I need her now."

Just as he pulled her into his embrace, she broke. Sam buried her head in his chest as sobs tore through her.

He knew, without a doubt, that no one had held her and let her cry this out. Nobody had been there for this little girl when she'd needed someone the most. Certainly not Stanley Donovan.

Years of emotions poured from her. The helpless feeling that swept through Brady only made him angrier with Sam's father and brother. And angry with himself. He didn't want Sam to hurt anymore, but he knew she would once all was said and done. So what right did he have to offer consolation now?

Had anyone been there for Sam when she'd needed them? Had Stanley grieved alone at the loss of his wife? Had he ever bothered to talk to Sam about the woman they both lost?

Brady wasn't sure what he would've done if he hadn't had Cade to lean on. And vice versa.

Minutes, maybe hours passed before Sam lifted her head. "I'm sorry for that."

Brady stroked her damp hair away from her face. "Crying? If you ask me, you're long overdue for an emotional meltdown."

"Did you have an emotional meltdown when your father passed?"

Images of throwing his glass of bourbon

against his bedroom wall and cursing everything and everyone around him filled his mind. "I did. People deal with death differently, though. But I had Cade and he had me."

She settled her cheek against his chest and wrapped her arm around his waist. "I guess I just needed to talk about her. You'd think I'd be used to life without her."

"She was your mother. I don't suspect you'll ever get used to being without her. I never have."

"The older I get, the harder it is to cope. I want to make the right choices in life, but I don't have anybody to give me advice or listen when I need to talk."

Brady kissed the top of her head. "You have me, Sam."

"For how long?"

He didn't bother answering.

How could he when he was unsure himself? What started out as a vendetta was slowly turning into something less sinister…at least where Samantha was concerned.

He gathered her close and prayed he would make the right decision for Sam. It was becoming more and more clear that Sam was going to get caught in the middle of this ugly war. It was only a matter of time before she became a casualty.

Brady ran a hand down his face and glanced back to the computer screen where he'd pulled up the San Francisco newspaper. The headline was still at the top of the page.

Easing back in his leather chair, he dialed his brother's office line.

The second his brother picked up, Brady said, "News sure got to the paper fast."

Cade sighed. "I can't believe they're already making the announcement."

The headline of the paper continued to stare back at him: Donovan Heir Takes Control.

The caption was complete with a picture of Miles with a smug grin.

Of course, this piece of news wasn't so new to Brady or Cade. They knew of the change in positions and the fact that Sam's father was retiring, thanks to the ever so clever snooping of their assistant, Abby.

It didn't matter who sat at the helm of the Donovan empire, Brady intended to crush them.

"This does take the Kauai property into a different direction," Cade said.

"Not necessarily," Brady countered. "We knew this announcement was coming. Actually, Sam may need me now more than ever."

"Had she mentioned this to you before?"

Brady shook his head. "No. Honestly, I doubt she knew until the last minute."

"So, she's nothing like the Donovan men?"

"They're polar opposites."

Cade let out a low whistle. "She's got you, doesn't she?"

"No." Brady shut down his laptop and came to his feet. "I think I'll make a call to the new CEO and offer my congratulations."

Cade laughed. "Let me know how it goes."

Brady disconnected the call and dialed

the Donovan offices, which happened to be close to his own San Francisco office. As he waited for the receptionist to put his call through, he gripped the receiver so tight he heard a slight crack.

"Miles Donovan."

Brady walked to the open patio doors and leaned against the door. He took great pleasure in being at the resort when his enemy on the other line had no clue.

"Miles. Brady Stone. I hear congratulations are in order."

"What do you want?"

"Just to say I hope you run the company better than your father did, for your sake."

"Is that a threat?" Miles demanded.

"Not at all." Brady breathed in the fresh salt water. "But just because you're in charge now doesn't mean you're going to be able to keep Lani Kaimana."

"Oh, I'll keep it, Stone. I'm not surprised you're trying to get that back after your father's death, but don't waste your time. I'm in charge now and I intend to keep everything that's mine."

Brady rubbed his smooth chin. "Well, good luck. You may be in charge, but I have an ace in the hole."

There was a slight pause on the other end and Brady wondered if Miles had heard him. He waited another few seconds.

"What's the matter, Miles? Worried?"

"You don't have squat. You're just running off at the mouth."

Brady shrugged, knowing the gesture

would come across in his tone. "Don't say I didn't warn you."

He hung up feeling better about the business, but sick to his stomach that he'd inadvertently used Sam.

Granted, from the beginning he'd always planned to use her as a conductor, but now that he'd done so, there was a sudden ache in his chest.

Brady turned away from the beauty of the white sand and frothy waves. He couldn't admit, even to himself, that the night with Sam had been too intense, too close to his heart. She'd somehow managed to chisel her way around the steel wall he'd erected around his emotions.

But what could be done now? He didn't

intend to back down and the damage was already done.

There was nothing to do but stay on target.

Twelve

Sam knew her father blamed her for the death of Beverly Donovan. If only he knew the impact his harsh words over the years had had on her.

She'd overheard him one night talking on the phone, to who she didn't know. He'd said if Bev hadn't been in such a hurry to get Sam to her dance class, she wouldn't have died.

Little did her father know, her mother had

been miserable for the past couple years of their marriage. Sam had discovered a journal her mother had kept. Within the thin pages, Bev had remarked time and again how she wished her husband would be as loving as he used to be, not work as much and pay more attention to Sam.

Sam had never picked up on the tension, if there was any, between her parents. Perhaps her mother would've left her father, perhaps not. Beverly Donovan was a strong, incredible woman and Sam wanted nothing more than to be just like her.

She already had the looks part down pat. But Sam wanted her mother's love of life; she wanted that vibrancy people saw when her mother would enter a room.

The chirping of her cell phone jarred her from her thoughts.

She didn't want to talk on the phone. She wanted to go see Brady. After two weeks of not being with him, she wanted to scream.

He'd told her Cade had to be out of the office for a few days, so Brady needed to return to San Francisco. Business was most definitely his life. Sam just hoped she was part of it, too.

Fastening her last gold hoop in her ear, Sam grabbed the phone from her nightstand and answered. "Hello."

"Sam."

Her excitement dropped. "Miles."

"Have you had any guests within the last week or so question you or the staff on the status of the resort?"

She rested a hand on her hip. "I haven't and the staff hasn't said anything. Why?"

"I'm almost certain that our main competitor is going to be making an appearance in an attempt to gain information to take the resort from us."

Horror filled Sam. "I won't let that happen."

"You may not be able to stop it. If something doesn't seem right, call me or Dad."

"Yeah, right. I can handle this, Miles. I will call you if I discover someone is pumping the staff for information, but I'd rather walk over hot coals than call Dad and explain I need his help."

"Samantha, be reasonable."

She sighed, not wanting to hear any more. "I have dinner plans. I have to go."

She hung up, pleased that Miles thought enough about her to include her in the business, but horrified at the thought of the beautiful place being taken from her. She'd come to think of this as her home, her life.

The knock on her door brought her back to the fact Brady was here. She was more than eager to see him again, make love to him again.

With one last glance in the mirror, Sam gave a nod of approval at her strapless white dress and gold T-strap sandals.

By the time she opened the door, she was as giddy as a schoolgirl.

"Hi," she greeted him.

His eyes raked over her, thrilling her and

making her want to forget the restaurant entirely.

"You look amazing," he whispered as he stepped over the threshold.

She'd barely gotten the door closed behind him before he spun her around and crushed his mouth to hers, wrapped her in his inviting embrace and made her knees turn to rubber.

She couldn't deny the fact he could make her forget her own name with just the touch of his lips.

But before she could even wrap her arms around his neck, he'd released her mouth, but not her body.

Dazed, Sam fluttered her lids and focused on him. "What was that for? To prove we're still combustible?"

Moist lips tilted up into a smile. "That was because you looked like you could use something to take your mind off whatever put that sad look in your eye."

Sam ran her hands over his crisp navy blue dress shirt, settling on his hard pecs. "Your tactics worked. But let's not discuss my personal issues. You're here now and I'm dying to get you naked again."

He kissed her once more. "You have the best ideas."

Needing to feel more of him, Sam moved her hands around to his back, lifted the hem of his shirt and slid her fingers along smooth, taut skin over well-toned muscle. A low moan escaped him, vibrating through his chest.

With a smile on her face, she glanced

up. Brady's eyes were closed. Sam placed small, short kisses on his neck, his chin, his jawline.

Suddenly, as if he couldn't take another second, Brady shoved her back against the door and lifted her dress. "You're a little minx," he growled.

With her body burning with need, she unbuttoned his shirt, slid it off his shoulders and made quick work on his belt, button and zipper.

Then, in one swift move Brady yanked her bikini panties. The tear pierced the air a split second before his hands found her most intimate spot. Spreading her legs wide, she granted him the access they both desperately needed.

He slid his finger over her center, penetrated

her, and she cried out. Bucking her hips, she held on to his bare shoulders.

"More. I need more."

Brady removed his hand, gripped her waist and lifted her so her body wedged between the door and his chest. "Wrap your legs around me."

The second her ankles locked behind his back, he drove into her. The fullness of him had her tilting her hips once again, eager to take all he could give.

Brady caged her body, leaving her no room to move. He was in complete control and she loved it. For once in her life, she liked being controlled by a man.

Hips pumping, warm breath ragged in her ear, Sam couldn't get enough of this potent man. He consumed her every fiber.

All too soon, she felt herself rise. She tried to increase the pace, wanting to get to her release, but Brady remained in charge.

"You're ready, aren't you?" he purred in her ear.

She couldn't piece together a response, instead she bit her lip and whimpered. Just then Brady moved in such a fast, frantic pace, Sam knew he must be close to his own release.

She turned her head, capturing his lips with her own. Tongues mimicked bodies as they rose together and held on for the climax.

They shuddered together, lips still fused as one. Nothing ever felt so intense, so perfect. Once the tremors ceased, Brady kissed her softly and eased back until her feet were once again on the carpet.

When he slid his hands up under her dress and removed the flimsy garment, Sam didn't protest. She didn't have the energy to. She'd never been taken in such an urgent way before, as if he couldn't live another minute without touching her.

The idea of being desired so much had her body humming for more all over again. What had she done to deserve this attention, this affection from such a remarkable man?

"We need to freshen up again," he murmured against her ear.

"But we have reservations."

He nipped at her chin. "I'll change them."

"I'm too tired," she protested as he scooped her up and headed toward the bathroom.

"Then I'll just have to do all the washing."

* * *

They dined in a romantic corner booth complete with candlelight. Brady, though, was having a hard time concentrating on anything other than the way Sam's bare shoulders looked in her strapless white dress. She'd pulled her hair up, leaving some tendrils down to dance around her tan shoulders.

She looked like a woman who had been thoroughly loved.

He'd seen the looks men had passed her way when they'd entered the restaurant. Jealousy didn't take over, though. No, Brady was glad they were looking. She was his, and he was proud of her.

Since when did he think of Samantha as his? If he didn't put a stop to these emotions he would fall for her.

"I've been thinking about going ahead with the spa," Sam said, drawing him back to the conversation.

"What?"

"I think we need to go ahead with the plans for the day spa." She rested her slender arms on the table. "I've already been in contact with a contractor. Would you mind looking over the plans he sent?"

"Not at all."

"Are you okay?" she asked.

Was he?

He faked a smile and nodded. "Fine. Just thinking about work. My brother is holding down the office until I return."

"You're lucky to have him."

Brady couldn't deny that. "We'll look over those plans after dinner. Moving ahead with this major renovation will put more of a rift between you and your father."

Sam's eyes misted. "Since he's not in charge anymore, I don't think he has room to criticize. Besides, my brother doesn't need to know every decision I make."

He reached up, covered her hand with his. "Your father hurt you with this new change in positions."

"I should've known I would never be considered for anything more than a hotel manager."

The way she put herself down and expected to be overlooked was heart-wrenching. How could he make things better for her and still gain control over the resort?

He couldn't. Which meant he had to choose.

Thirteen

Samantha held the stick, stared at the two pink lines and didn't know if she wanted to throw up or jump up and down. But it had only been two weeks since they'd slept together. And they hadn't used a condom. The realization hit her hard.

A baby.

Brady's baby.

She sat on the edge of her bathtub and took

deep, calming breaths. Okay, the breaths were deep, but not calming.

Other than being one day late for her period, which was always regular, she had no symptoms.

She placed a shaky hand on her still-flat abdomen. More signs would come soon enough.

What would Brady think? They hadn't even spoken the three most important words that should be spoken *before* making a baby.

Even though she did love him. She wouldn't be this deep into a relationship if she didn't. She wouldn't have opened up about her mother, her worries as a businesswoman, if she hadn't fallen for him.

When the burning of fresh tears threatened, Sam came to her feet, placed the stick on the edge of the counter and went to dress for work.

She'd had to go to the pharmacy early this morning for the test and pray that no one recognized her. That's all she needed was for news to travel back to her father, her brother or worse, Brady, before she could tell him.

How would she break this life-altering news?

She hoped Brady was happy, but she understood if he didn't want a family. He was, after all, a businessman with a chaotic schedule. How would a wife and baby fit into the mix?

And who's to say he would even want to marry her, she thought as she grabbed her Kate Spade handbag. Honestly, she didn't want Brady to marry her because he felt obligated to. Marriages that started out of obligation usually ended in disaster.

They were still getting to know each other. Actually, they hadn't even spoken about how far this relationship had progressed.

Did Brady even consider them a couple? Was he just with her while he stayed on the island for business?

She stepped onto the elevator, and because the doors shut leaving her all alone, she placed a hand on her flat tummy and grinned.

"I love you already," she whispered.

If Brady took the news well and was excited, Samantha would have to make more life-altering decisions.

Working under Miles would probably not be good in the long run.

224 SEDUCING THE ENEMY'S DAUGHTER

And even though she hated to give up Lani Kaimana, she knew making a life with her baby and Brady would be better in the long run.

After all, how could she work fourteen-hour days and take care of a little one?

God, all the what-ifs swirled around in her head as she passed through the lobby.

Employees nodded and smiled, and Samantha wondered if they knew. Could they tell she was going to be a mother? Could they see it in the silly smile she knew she wore on her face?

She needed to speak to Brady as soon as possible. She couldn't wait to tell someone the news. But this was also the one time in her life she'd dreaded. How would she cope with a child without her own mother? Who would give her motherly advice?

A lump formed in Sam's throat at the thought of going through this without her best friend.

God, what an emotional wreck she was. This pregnancy thing really did take a toll on emotions. Hadn't she just been smiling five seconds ago?

She headed down the hallway to check on the progress of the spa. The contractor had started on the renovations last week and Sam was already hearing the buzz about guests who were eager to return.

"There you are."

Sam turned to the male voice and was shocked to see her brother.

"Miles," she greeted as she gripped her purse tighter. "What are you doing here?"

"I came to check things out," Miles said.

Sam clasped her hands together instead of balling them into a fist like she wanted to do. "You mean to check up on me."

"I'm looking out for my property, Samantha."

She quirked a brow at him. "I certainly hope you don't consider this your property. If I recall, I'm the one that has been here busting my butt since we acquired it and you just slid into dad's seat."

"Let's not get petty," Miles suggested. "Could we talk in your office?"

Sam hesitated a split second before she stalked off, leading the way. The sooner she found out what he wanted and got him out of here, the sooner she could track down Brady and see what their future held.

Because she wanted to keep the upper hand for as long as she could, Sam stepped behind her neatly organized desk and sat her bag at her feet, but did not take a seat until her door was firmly closed and Miles was seated across from her.

"Now," she said getting comfortable in her leather chair. "What is this impromptu visit about?"

Miles eased forward in his chair. "As I told you on the phone, I have reason to believe one of our main competitors is here or will be on his way."

"Yes," Sam agreed, trying to keep the irritation out of her tone. "And, as I told you, I can handle it and I would call you if I thought something was up."

"I'm also taking this opportunity to check out the whole resort," Miles went on as if she hadn't spoken. "I was shocked when I heard you were going ahead with some rather expensive plans. We really don't have spa money in our budget."

Deep breaths, she told herself, deep breaths. In, out. "We will have a nice return on our investment. Trust me. And if there was a problem that I couldn't handle, such as a competitor coming in, I would've called you."

Miles stared at her for what seemed like eternity before nodding. "Let me see what's going on with the spa area."

"Fine." She came to her feet. "But we have to hurry. I have a busy schedule."

She opened her door with a jerk, the not-so-subtle way of letting her brother know she was not happy. After she gestured for him to go ahead, she closed and locked her door behind her.

A bit of her tension eased as they entered the open lobby and Brady stepped off the elevator looking extremely sexy in khaki shorts and a green polo.

She turned to her brother. "Excuse me just one minute."

With a smile and a quick stride, Sam made her way across the marble floor. "Hey, are you going out?"

Brady closed the gap between them. "I

was going for a walk on the beach. Care to join me?"

"You don't know how much I'd love to, but I have something I have to take care of first." She stood on her toes and kissed him on the cheek. "I'll come find you later."

"What the hell is going on?"

Samantha jumped around at the booming sound of Miles's voice. "Excuse me?"

"Miles," Brady said.

Sam threw a look over her shoulder. "You know my brother?"

"Oh, he knows me all right," Miles confirmed. "He probably knew you, too, before he ever stepped foot here."

Samantha's heartbeat kicked up. From the tension surrounding her, the tone in the two male voices and the look of murder in both their eyes, she had a feeling this scene was about to get really ugly.

"Let's all go back to my office," she said quietly.

"I'd like to talk to you alone," Brady said.

Miles laughed. "I'm sure you would, Stone. Let me guess, you've been working my sister in the romance department trying to get in on some company secrets?"

Her once-beating heart dropped. "What?"

Brady took her arm and turned her around. "Sam, please, let me talk to you alone."

The pleading look in his eyes made her want to go with him, to hear what exactly was going on. But the logical side of her knew whatever he had to say could possibly destroy them.

Oh, God. The baby.

No, she could not get upset. She had to remain calm. There was someone depending on her now.

"Don't listen to him," Miles said. "He's a liar."

Sam turned back around. "You have no right to talk to me about liars. You and Father kept secrets from me from day one on this job and if I want to talk to Brady, I will."

"Do you know who he really is?" Miles asked.

"His father used to own this resort." Miles paused when the elevator dinged and a couple stepped off. "Let's step over here out of ear-shot of our guests."

Shaky legs carried Sam around the corner with the men. They stood in an empty hall-way that led to the conference room she'd wanted transformed into a day care. But suddenly, nothing mattered but the truth.

"Has Brady told you he intends to steal this property back from us?" Miles continued.

"I'm not stealing anything," Brady said in a cold, flat tone. "I'm simply taking back what my father used as the foundation of his enterprise and your father stole at a moment of weakness."

Sam's head was spinning. She held up her hands. "Wait. Brady's family owned this before we bought it?"

"Stole it," Brady corrected.

"How could we steal it?" she questioned.

Brady rested his hands on his hips. "Ask your father and brother."

A wave of dizziness swept over her. Sam

settled her back against the wall and prayed she wouldn't pass out.

"Just tell me one thing," she said. "Did you know who I was before you came here?"

"You're his ace in the hole. Right, Brady?" Miles asked. "I assume when you called me the other day you were referring to my sister."

God, this wasn't happening. This was just another cruel trick fate was playing on her. How could she have been so blindsided, so in need of affection that she'd completely let all common sense dissipate?

Samantha wanted out of this mess. She wanted to go back to this morning to when she'd first discovered she and Brady may have a solid future together. She wanted this nightmare to be just that…a nightmare. But she knew she wouldn't be waking up anytime soon. This was reality and now she had to deal with it.

"You called my brother?"

Before or after we made love, she wanted to add. Made love. No, that's not what they'd done at all. Suddenly everything she thought they'd shared was tainted by lies.

"You had this planned from the beginning, didn't you?" she whispered because tears clogged her throat.

Brady's eyes held hers. "I came here to confront a Sam Donovan, who I thought was a man, so yes, in a sense."

"Convenient I turned out to be a woman." Sam's stomach turned, bile rose in her throat. "So you decided to use me."

Brady didn't bother to answer seeing as

how she'd made an accusation, not asked a question.

"Can we talk?" Brady whispered, his coal-like eyes searching her face.

"I think I've heard enough." Samantha pushed off the wall and willed the nausea to cease. "I'm going to my room. I want both of you out of my hotel by the end of the day. Miles, I'll speak with you later regarding my status with the company."

"What does that mean?" he asked.

"It means I'm not sure I can continue to work for you."

She walked slowly away from the men. How could she continue to work for Miles when she was having the enemy's baby? Miles—and her father—wouldn't understand.

The excitement she'd felt earlier had

vanished, but the one thing that remained was the fact a piece of her was still in love with Brady. Well, the Brady she thought she knew.

How could such a loving man be so conniving, so vindictive?

Samantha barely made it back to her suite and into the bathroom before she fell to her knees and threw up.

Fourteen

By the time Monday rolled around, Brady was more than ready to battle with Miles over Lani Kaimana. He was just glad Cade was going to the meeting with the attorneys he'd had scheduled over another property. No way could he have gone and tried to discuss business today.

Brady's temper had still not settled back down from the hurt he'd seen in Sam's eyes caused by Miles's ill-timed interference. Not that there would've been a good time, he thought.

And how could he place the blame solely on Miles? Wasn't Brady the one who'd set out to seduce Sam? To gain her trust and access all the company's dirty laundry to use against them?

But, dammit, he hadn't known he'd come to actually care for her.

Now the need to take away everything that mattered to Stanley and Miles was stronger than ever. Everything they cared about would become his.

After all, they'd taken away a portion of his father's legacy and Samantha.

Would Sam see his way of thinking? She, more than anyone else, knew the kind of men her father and brother were. She also knew the kind of pain that came along with losing a parent and how you just wanted to lay blame with someone.

Hadn't she blamed herself for the death of her mother? Surely she would see Brady's side of things once she cooled off and could think rationally.

God, was he practicing his speech to her or trying to convince himself?

Sitting in his San Francisco office, Brady tried to catch up on his work, but the thought of Cade with the attorneys right now only made him anxious to move forward with building back their father's company.

He glanced at the digital clock on the lower right-hand corner of his computer screen. The meeting had only been going on ten minutes, and that was if they got started on time.

Hell, who was he kidding? He couldn't even concentrate on the new property they were obtaining. All he kept thinking of was Sam's tearful recollection of her childhood and the fact she wanted Lani Kaimana just as bad as he and his brother did, but for totally different reasons.

He thought of the way she'd made love with him, pouring all her emotions into their intimacy. The way she'd opened up about her feelings growing up and losing her mother.

But most of all, he couldn't stop thinking about the hurtful look in her eyes when she'd found out the truth.

He would find a way to make this right, to make sure she got everything she ever wanted. No matter what he had to barter or pay, he'd make sure Samantha stayed on at the resort. He no longer wanted it for himself.

And that thought made Brady freeze.

That statement confirmed his love. He'd only recently discovered the emotion, but wasn't sure how real it was. Now he knew. How could he have not seen the whole picture until now?

True, he'd started this vendetta out of revenge and he still wanted to make the Donovans pay, but somewhere along the way, obtaining the property turned into making Sam happy. Truly happy for once in her life.

Brady knew what he was about to do was perhaps the dumbest business move he'd ever made. Hell, forget *business* move, this was the dumbest move—period.

He was tired of sitting around moping, tired of being alone and worrying about her. So he got into his Navigator and decided to do something.

Twenty minutes later, he pulled up in front of the Donovans' office building and killed the engine. If Sam knew what he was about to do, she'd probably be more furious—if that was even possible. But Sam didn't know, and as far as he was concerned, she didn't need to know.

More than ready to confront any and/or all of the Donovans, Brady stepped out into the sultry summer heat and made his way into the cool, air-conditioned building. Stepping into the lion's den didn't sit well with him, but at this point he'd go head-to-head with the devil himself if he could prevent any more pain from slipping into Sam's life.

"Can I help you?" The petite, elderly receptionist greeted him with a smile. Obviously she didn't know who he was.

Brady returned her smile and stepped forward. "I'd like to see Miles Donovan, please. I'm afraid I don't have an appointment, but this is a pressing matter."

The woman shuffled around the papers on her desk and looked over what Brady assumed to be Miles's schedule. "He's free for the next twenty minutes. Let me make sure he's up for a visitor. May I tell him your name?"

"Brady Stone."

He had to give this lady credit, her smile

barely faltered before she picked up her phone and dialed the extension.

Brady glanced around the cold black-and-chrome office. There was nothing warm and inviting about the waiting area, nothing that greeted the clients other than the receptionist.

Black leather chairs, chrome-and-glass tables with a few *GQ* magazines, no plants, no pictures on the white walls, not even an area rug over the dark hardwood floors.

"He'll see you now, Mr. Stone."

Turning his attention back to the woman, Brady smiled. "Thank you."

"His office is the last door on the right," she said, motioning down the long, narrow hall.

Even though the door was closed, Brady

didn't bother knocking. Rude, yes, but considering the man on the other side of the door, Brady didn't care.

"Hell must have frozen over for you to darken my office." Miles came to his feet, motioning for Brady to have a seat across from the large oak desk. "Either that, or you're here on my sister's behalf."

Brady didn't take the chair that was offered. He'd rather stand. Getting comfortable in this office wasn't likely.

"I want to call a truce," he said. "Samantha doesn't need to be caught in the middle of this feud."

Miles shoved his jacket back from his waist and rested his hands on his hips. "You have a lot of nerve, Stone. You tried to seduce my sister, when she had no idea who you were, in order to gain information about this company and now you're worried about her welfare?"

Brady swallowed, ignoring the guilt that crept up. "I'm here to make sure she doesn't get hurt any more."

"I don't intend to hurt her. And I suggest you move on. The resort and my sister will no longer be your concern."

"On the contrary," Brady said. "Sam and Lani Kaimana are very much my concern."

Miles chuckled. "You can't be serious about pursuing Sam. You used her as leverage to get back Lani Kaimana."

Anger bubbled inside Brady, but he pushed it down for Sam's sake. "Well, now I'm not using her for anything. You may find this hard to believe, but I care for her."

The muscle in Miles's jaw clenched. "Care? I doubt you care for her. Although I'm sure you care about everything we own, so maybe you'll continue to charm her. You may even resort to begging in order to get her to come back. Whatever it takes in the name of business. Right, Stone?"

How on earth could Miles think so little of his sister? Had their father been so cruel to Sam that Miles could just toss her aside?

Brady clenched his fists at his side. "I don't care what you think. I'm only concerned with Sam."

Without another word, he exited from the office. Maybe the meeting hadn't gone so well, but what had he expected? The Donovan men weren't known for their ability to get along with others. Perhaps that's why they were failing so miserably at their business dealings as of late.

But he would put forth an effort only for Sam.

Brady called Abby and informed her that he'd be spending the rest of the day out of the office. He also left a voice mail for Cade to call after he'd finished with the attorney.

He needed to clear his head. No way could he work with all the anger and rage that flooded through him. Added to that, he had to go back to Kauai, force Sam to hear his side and plead for forgiveness. She may never, ever forgive him, but he had to make sure she understood his actions.

Brady's head fell back against the seat. He couldn't pinpoint the exact time he fell in love with Sam. And he *was* in love with her.

There wasn't a doubt in his mind. He'd never felt this way about another woman. Never wanted to be their protector, their provider, their lifetime partner.

Lifetime. His heartbeat quickened, from excitement and eagerness—and a slice of fear.

How could he go on if she chose to never forgive him? He could never love anyone as much as he loved Samantha.

He'd never backed down from a fight and he didn't intend to start now. Not when it truly mattered.

Brady exited his Lincoln and headed up the narrow steps to his suburban home. He wanted a chance at a relationship. He wanted to start off strong and grow from there. He wanted to give her the life she'd never had, a life she deserved, full of love and happiness.

With plans already forming in his head, Brady unlocked his front door and prepared the speech in his head.

Fifteen

Dread, sadness and loneliness enveloped Sam each time she stepped into her childhood home. How had she managed not to go insane all the years she'd lived here?

The marble floors gleamed, the chandeliers sparkled, sending a vast array of shapes and colors down and, as usual, not a thing was out of place. No shoes by the front door, no keys lying haphazardly on the secretary inside the foyer. No sign of life.

The house was just as it had been after her mother's passing.

Sam rubbed her arms against the chilly aura and ventured on. She should've called ahead, but she didn't want any more harsh words than necessary with her father.

Stanley Donovan was in the first place Sam looked…the same room he'd lived in all her life. His office.

She stood in the doorway, staring across the room to the man who was her father, but had always seemed more of a stranger than anything.

He still used the same old oak desk. His floor-to-ceiling bookcases provided the backdrop, stretching the length of the wall.

He was no doubt in his element.

But instead of the robust, domineering man she'd recalled, Stanley looked old. His hair had gone from silver to mostly white and had started retreating from his forehead. His hands, which held on to a file probably containing his latest stock report, were wrinkled.

He rubbed his head with a weathered hand and Sam couldn't help but feel pity for him. All his life he'd concentrated on making money, working the next deal, but he'd missed everything that mattered. His family.

Samantha settled her hand on her stomach and entered the room.

"Dad."

Stanley jerked his head, dropping the file onto the neatly organized desk. "Samantha. What brings you here?"

She stepped farther into the den. "We need to talk. Actually, I need to talk and I need you to listen."

"Sounds important." He crossed his hands over his small, round belly and leaned back in his chair. "Does this have to do with business?"

She laughed, taking a seat across from him. "Everything always comes back to business with you, doesn't it? I guess in a way, what I have to say does center around business."

"Miles told me you turned in your resignation."

"Yes, but that's not what I want to discuss." Sam willed her cowardly nerves away and focused on the mission she came for. "I want to know why you always treated Miles different from me."

"I don't know what you're talking about," he said. "And I can't believe you'd even ask such a childish question."

"Childish? You know good and well you treat the two of us differently. You always have. Since Mom's death, you act like I'm a stray off the street that you were burdened with."

Stanley sighed. "If I have treated you different from Miles, it's only because I was trying to do what your mother would've wanted."

Confused, Sam asked, "What?"

"Beverly never wanted you to be part of the family business. She didn't want you to be swallowed up in all of this like I've always been. She knew Miles always wanted to be involved, so she didn't say too much about him. But you…" Stanley shook his head. "You were special. You were like an angel when you came to us. All that blond hair and those wide blue eyes. You were an image of your mother and I couldn't love you more."

The steel wall Sam had built up in defense before arriving here today suddenly crumbled. "But why were you so cruel to me after her death? Why did you always push me further and further away? Even now, you can hardly look at me."

He looked down, wiping both eyes with his forefinger and thumb. "It still hurts. Looking at you," he said softly. "I just see her. I know it's a poor excuse, but it's the truth."

Unsure of how to respond, Sam did the only thing she could think of. She came to her feet and went to her father. Wrapping her arms around his broad shoulders, she kissed the top of his head.

"I'm sorry," she whispered. "I'm so sorry you were grieving all that time and I was to blame."

He wrapped his hand around her arm. "No, Sam, you weren't to blame. I was. I tried placing blame everywhere but where it belonged. Had I been more of a husband, more active in my family's life, perhaps your mother wouldn't have been in a hurry that day. I know I should've been there for you, but I just couldn't. Looking at your face each day only added to the torment of knowing I'd never see her again. I devoted my life to my work, in the hopes of getting away from the pain."

Sam tightened her hold. "I see her face, too, each time I look in the mirror."

"I'm sorry if you thought I was pushing

you away. The truth is, I'm proud of you. I'm proud of the woman you've become and I know your mother would be, as well."

Sam's heart swelled as a warm tear trickled down her cheek. This was the father she'd waited so many years to have. This was the moment she'd longed for, cried for.

"I've said some hurtful things to you," he went on. "If I could take them back, I would. You've accomplished so much in such a short time. Not only are you successful in business, but you take the time to enjoy life. I'm glad you didn't follow in my footsteps. I'm afraid Miles has, though."

Sam stepped back. "He has a stubborn streak, but he's a good man. You did just fine."

Stanley looked up with moist, red eyes.

"Maybe, but I need him to know working himself to the bone won't make him happy. I want him to take time to enjoy life, too."

"Then talk to him," she suggested with a squeeze. "He probably longs for a one-on-one conversation about something other than business just like I did."

"I will. Can we have a new beginning?"

Sam smiled, with tears in her eyes and a hand on her belly. "Yes. I'd like that."

She couldn't tell her father yet. No one knew about the baby. She was ten weeks pregnant now and although some of the employees had noticed her getting sick on occasion, she'd always come up with a lie.

Sam didn't stay at her father's home long, but promised to visit often. The weighty burden of their strained relationship she'd carried in with her no longer existed when she left. At least now she knew. She knew her father had grieved all this time and that he hadn't hated her, he simply didn't know how to deal with his emotions.

As Sam made her way to the airport, she knew her next step should be to contact Brady about the baby. Even though he was a lying, coldhearted bastard, he was still going to be a father and Samantha didn't have the heart not to tell him.

After all, she'd essentially lost both parents. How could she deny her own child?

Brady paced in Samantha's suite at Lani Kaimana. Luckily he'd been let in by one of the maids who'd seen Brady and Sam together often enough that she knew they'd been seeing each other. Fortunately for him, the maid had no idea Samantha probably hated his guts right now.

Where the hell was she?

He was told she'd left yesterday for a personal reason, but was due back at the resort today. He was also told she had resigned and was only going to be manager for a few more days. So now he had to wait and find out what the hell she was doing. And why she was giving up on something she loved so much.

Tugging off his suit jacket, Brady draped it over the back of the sofa. He unbuttoned his sleeves, rolled them up and unfastened the top button of his shirt.

Might as well get comfortable, he thought as he seated himself on the couch.

A folder with the name of a local doctor stamped on the front drew Brady's attention to the squatty, glass coffee table.

When he opened the file, something fell into his lap.

A picture. Not just any picture, he thought as he studied it. A picture of an ultrasound.

Because he really couldn't tell what he was looking at, he glanced at the papers in the folder.

No. This couldn't be.

Samantha was ten weeks pregnant? *Pregnant?*

Brady did some quick figuring in his head. That meant she knew she was expecting his child when they'd seen each other last.

Brady dropped the file onto the table and

came to his feet, still clutching the picture of his unborn baby.

Was she going to tell him? Did she plan on keeping up this preposterous job with a chaotic schedule while pregnant? Obviously that's why she was giving up the resort.

Did Miles know? Did anybody?

The idea of Samantha keeping this secret to herself, going through this alone, infuriated him.

At some point she'd have to shove her pride aside and ask for help. And, dammit, he'd be the one to give it to her.

The buzz from a key card at the suite door had him jerking around.

Samantha stepped in and jumped. "Brady! What are you doing here?"

For a moment, he could do nothing but

stare. He didn't know what he expected. A big belly? No, that didn't come until later. But she did look beautiful. Her skin had a healthy, tanned tone, indicating she'd probably taken advantage of the sandy beach only steps away.

She looked sexy in the simple white sundress that stopped just above her knees. Her hair was down, the way he liked it, spilling over her shoulders, giving her an innocent look.

And wasn't that what killed him the most? She had been innocent in this whole thing.

"You look good," he said, once he got passed the lump in his throat.

"You have two minutes to say whatever it is you came for. I have to meet my father in

San Francisco." She sat down her overnight bag and purse and crossed her arms. "Go."

"Can we have a seat and talk?"

"No."

Brady held up the picture. "Fine. When were you going to tell me about this?"

He had to give her credit, she didn't even bat an eye before she responded.

"The same day I found out the father of my baby was a conniving jerk. Funny, I didn't get around to it."

She moved from the doorway, shoving her bags aside with her foot and letting the door slam behind her. Striding across the room, she didn't even look at him as she went into her bedroom.

Brady followed.

"Were you ever going to tell me?" he asked.

Samantha reached into her drawers and started pulling clothes out and piling them on the bed. "Yes."

"You're sure?"

She stopped, a pile of silky bras dangling from her hands. "I'm not a liar. And I wouldn't deprive my child from knowing its parents."

At least that was something.

"I came back because you need to listen to me," he told her.

She rounded on him, hands on her hips. "I don't have to do anything. What I need to do right now is pack because I'm currently unemployed."

"Then come work for me."

He wasn't surprised at her outburst of laughter, but that didn't negate the fact that her dismissal hurt.

"You're kidding, right? I wouldn't work for you for any amount of money you offered."

"Then do it for the baby." He searched her face, hoping she'd see the love in his eyes. "Don't shut me out, not now. Not when I've fallen in love with you."

She stepped back, placed a hand out to the bed and eased down. "Don't. Don't throw that word out like you mean it. I won't be fooled again."

Putting everything he had on the line, his pride, his heart, Brady squatted down in front of her and took her hands.

"Do you think I'd come back if I didn't care for you?" he asked. "I'm not here for the baby, I didn't even know until I saw the file. I'm here because I realized you were more important than any resort, any business deal."

She tugged her hands free and wiped her damp eyes. "That may be true, but I can't trust what you say anymore. I won't be misled or used again."

She came to her feet, causing him to take a step back.

"Now," she said with her chin high, "I need to be alone. Please don't call me. I'll let you know all about the baby's doctor's appointments and keep you up-to-date, but other than that, I don't want any contact with you."

Brady fisted his hands at his side and swallowed. He wouldn't push, not when her condition was so delicate, but he wouldn't give up. Ever.

"You'll see how much I love you," he promised as he kissed her lightly on the cheek.

Without another word, and with a heavy heart, Brady left.

Sixteen

Without Sam's bright, sunny smile to fill the building, fill his life, Brady's days were lifeless.

Just as they'd been before she'd entered his life.

Of course, he hadn't known how boring and empty his life had been, but now that he'd experienced love, well, nothing mattered if he had to live without.

He'd caused the damage by getting the ball rolling the second he decided to get closer to Sam. And now he had to do some major work to undo what he'd done.

A week had come and gone since he'd seen her in Kauai. Brady didn't recall a longer seven days in his life.

As he shut down his computer and grabbed his suit jacket from the back of his leather chair, his desk line rang.

"Brady Stone."

"Brady, this is Stanley Donovan." The elderly man cleared his throat. "I'm with Sam at St. Mary's Hospital. I stopped by her house and she was having some stomach pains. We're waiting to see the doctor. I don't know what the personal nature of your relationship is now, but I thought you'd want to know."

Before Brady could process what the old man had said, much less ask questions, Stanley had hung up.

Fear, guilt and just plain terror ripped through him as he made a mad dash down the stairs and out to his SUV. He didn't bother saying anything to Abby or Cade—there was no time.

Was the baby okay? Was Sam? She had to be so scared. Brady was grateful Stanley had thought to call.

God, she couldn't lose the baby. Brady's hands tightened on the steering wheel as he cursed the weekend rush-hour traffic.

Arguments, betrayals, secrets, none of it mattered now. All that mattered was Sam and the baby. They had to be all right. They *had* to.

The usual twenty-minute drive to the hospital ended up taking nearly an hour. After handing his keys over to the valet driving attendant, Brady raced inside the main glass doors and up to the information desk.

"Samantha Donovan," he said breathlessly. "She was brought in a little over an hour ago. Probably in maternity."

The young receptionist glanced to her computer, typed in the name and drew her brows together. "She's in triage—third floor."

Brady took the elevator and prayed everything would be fine. Damn, he couldn't lose his future.

"Brady."

As he stepped off the elevator, he turned to the sound of his name. Brady nearly wept with relief when he saw Stanley strutting toward him.

"Where is she?" he demanded.

Stanley nodded with his head. "Follow me."

Allowing Sam's father to lead the way, Brady sent up another prayer that everything was all right. But he braced himself for the worst.

"How is she?" Brady asked as they walked back through the sterile hall.

"She's says she's fine."

"What are the doctors saying?"

Stanley stopped in front of the sliding-glass door. "She spoke with them alone and she won't tell me what's wrong. She did reassure me that she was indeed fine and she got teary when I told her you were on your way."

Brady didn't know what to make of that other than the fact Stanley obviously didn't know about the baby. But he did know being in a hospital was not helping his nerves any.

The antiseptic scent made him want to gag, to run away and avoid the hurt of losing someone else he loved with every fiber of his being. He hadn't been here since his father's illness.

Thankfully before he got even more carried away with his thoughts, he slid the door open, stepped into her room and shoved the pale blue curtain aside.

Brady's heart nearly stopped when she turned to look at him. Her eyes were red, puffy, her color was off. The oversize hospital gown swallowed up her petite frame.

She was still the most beautiful sight he'd ever laid eyes on.

And wasn't this ironic? The very man he'd set out to destroy was now the crutch he may very well have to lean on during this time.

Brady moved to one side of the bed and took her hand. "Sam, are you all right?"

Her misty eyes darted over his shoulder. "Dad, would you give us a minute?"

"I'll give you five," Stanley said. "But after that, I want to know what is going on."

A smile played at the corners of her mouth. "I promise."

The sliding door opened, then closed, once again silencing the chaos on the other side.

Brady bent, kissed her head and inhaled her sweet aroma. "God, Sam, please tell me…"

"Shh, it's all right," she assured him. "I'm

sorry my father scared you. The baby is fine and so am I."

"May I sit here?" he asked as his hip rested on the edge of the bed.

"Please."

Brady waited for her to say something. He couldn't imagine why she told her father she was fine when clearly she wasn't. What had caused her to cry so much the tip of her little nose was red?

He couldn't take the silence. "Your father said you got upset when he told you he called me."

She glanced down to her hands as they toyed with the hem of the bleached-white blanket. "Yes."

"Do you want me to go?"

"No." She continued to work her shaky

hands. "I just… I don't know how to tell you this. Not with the tension between us and the harsh words."

Brady's chest tightened as he lifted her chin with his index finger. "Forget about that for now. I'm going crazy here. What's wrong?"

"Twins," she blurted out before shielding her face with her hands and bursting into tears.

Twins? The word registered in Brady's head. *Two* babies.

A grin split across his face as a chuckle bubbled its way up. "Sam," he said, easing her hands down. "Why are you so upset?"

She looked up, sniffed. "Are you laughing?"

Squeezing her delicate, wet hands between

his own, he kissed her loudly on the mouth. "God, you have no idea what had been going through my mind. But, two babies? How could I not be happy?"

Brady covered her mouth with his hand, then slid his fingers around to caress her cheek. "Sam, I love you."

"I know. I saw your face when you came in." She smiled through teary eyes. "You were frightened and I know you wouldn't have been if you didn't care. I guess I should've listened to my heart days ago."

Relief swept through him. "I'm glad your heart knew the right answer."

"I spoke with Miles today," she told him. "He told me the two of you are considering joining forces with the resort."

Brady shrugged. "I wanted to do something

to ease your pain, to make sure you didn't have to choose sides and you could have control over the dealings with Lani Kaimana."

"That's another reason I knew you loved me," she confessed.

Brady squeezed her hands. "So why did you have pain? Did the doctors say?"

"Because with two babies, my uterus is stretching faster, so I was cramping a lot."

"I still can't believe it," he muttered. "Why didn't you tell your father?"

"We're just getting back to a father-daughter relationship, so I haven't filled him in on too much of my personal life."

"I noticed the tension that normally surrounded the two of you wasn't there." Brady moved his hand from her cheek back to her hand. "I know I don't deserve a second chance, but I want to be a part of my babies' lives."

"Are you saying you only want to be in their lives?"

His heart nearly leaped through his chest. "No. I'd love to be in your life again, Sam. I want so much from you, it scares me. I want you to be my wife. Say yes."

Sam sat up straighter, reached to touch his cheek. "Brady, I love you. Yes, I'll be your wife."

Epilogue

One month later, subtle waves rippled onto the beach as the vibrant orange sun set beyond the water.

Sam couldn't believe she was marrying Brady on the beach in front of their resort. He looked so handsome barefoot in his khaki linen pants and white button-up shirt. She'd wanted a simple wedding and when he'd suggested the location, she knew they couldn't begin their life together at a better spot.

"I now pronounce you husband and wife," the priest said. "You may kiss your bride, Mr. Stone."

Brady's eyes focused on her lips as his mouth spread into a grin. "My pleasure."

He kissed her slowly, passionately. Their first kiss as Mr. and Mrs. Stone.

Brady eased back, then whispered in her ear, "You look beautiful."

Sam had chosen a pale pink strapless chiffon dress that stopped just below her knees. She wore her mother's diamond earrings and necklace, a present from her father.

Rising on her tiptoes, she whispered, "Let's break the news."

"Okay."

The priest announced the new couple and Cade and Sam's father applauded. Sam hugged her dad and kissed him on the cheek.

"I have an announcement to make," she said, clasping her husband's hand. All eyes were on her as the quivering in her belly took control. "You know how we Donovans and Stones don't do anything halfway."

She smiled at their nods. "Well, there will be two babies in the spring, not just one."

Stanley slapped Brady on the back, hugged Samantha. "A new legacy with two of the strongest families. I'd say that's a great way to start a life together."

"I couldn't have said it better myself," Brady announced as he looked into the eyes of his bride.

* * * * *

Discover Pure Reading Pleasure with

**Visit the Mills & Boon website for all
the latest in romance**

🌹 **Buy** all the latest
releases, backlist
and eBooks

🌹 **Find out** more
about our authors
and their books

🌹 **Join** our community
and chat to authors
and other readers

🌹 **Free** online reads
from your favourite
authors

🌹 **Win** with our
fantastic online
competitions

🌹 **Sign** up for our
free monthly
eNewsletter

🌹 **Tell us** what you think
by signing up to our
reader panel

🌹 **Rate** and review
books with our star
system

www.millsandboon.co.uk

 Follow us at twitter.com/millsandboonuk

 Become a fan at facebook.com/romancehq